THE YOUTHENING

"Widdick appears to have Korsakov's Syndrome," I told him, "but it's complicated by a delusion of a past life that he couldn't have lived."

The director frowned and said, "There's more to it." He handed me a photograph. "What does this suggest to you?"

The picture looked like Widdick but older, and I said so. "It's as if his hairline had receded."

"Widdick has been here for fourteen years," the director said. "That picture was taken when he arrived."

I laughed. "Don't ask me to believe that he's growing younger . . ."

RETRO LIVES

LEE GRIMES

AVON BOOKS • NEW YORK

RETRO LIVES is an original publication of Avon Books. This work has never before appeared in book form. This work is a novel. Any similarity to actual persons or events is purely coincidental.

AVON BOOKS
A division of
The Hearst Corporation
1350 Avenue of the Americas
New York, New York 10019

Copyright © 1993 by Lee Grimes
Cover illustration by Robert Wood
Published by arrangement with the author
Library of Congress Catalog Card Number: 92-97002
ISBN: 0-380-76913-1

First AvoNova Printing: March 1993

AVONOVA TRADEMARK REG. U.S. PAT. OFF. AND IN OTHER COUNTRIES, MARCA REGISTRADA, HECHO EN U.S.A.

Printed in the U.S.A.

RA   10 9 8 7 6 5 4 3 2 1

To Jeffrey M. Grimes,
oenologist and litterateur

Chapter One

To commemorate the five hundredth anniversary of the birth of Robert Widdick, Jason has asked that members of the family receive copies of selected documents held in the archives. We can forget the fanciful legends we learned in childhood. The documents need no embroidery to show Robert's indomitable spirit and his resourcefulness in confronting obstacles that we can scarcely imagine. A reliable portrayal of his early problems comes from an account by the doctor who was the first to sense them.

—GABRIEL (D) CHEN, ARCHIVIST

From the Journal of Milton Kleiffer, M.D. (1985)

Fools might envy Robert Widdick. His children call him a monster. I fear that he is damned.

His family will not allow me to publish his case history, not even a discreet account in a medical journal referring to an anonymous Patient X.

Investigation would surely follow, and sensationalists would publicize a miracle while ignoring the cost. My diary strains ethics to ease my frustration.

When I have forgotten my birthday I will still remember the date we met: September 4, 1984. Ours is a small private hospital, in which I began work on that Monday. We care for schizophrenics, manic-depressives, anorectics, alcoholics, amnesiacs, and Widdick. The director asked me to see Widdick first.

"This will lift your eyebrows," the director said, "but I want you to interview him without seeing his file. I want an evaluation completely uninfluenced by the opinions of others, or by what may or may not be facts on record. Develop his background yourself. See if you can come up with a diagnosis. Afterwards I'll go over his case with you."

I shrugged as I agreed. The diagnosis of most mental disturbances is straightforward, although patients can be clever in their lies.

A male nurse wearing a white jacket and pants brought Widdick to my office. Widdick was of medium height, powerfully built, with a full head of straight brown hair parted on the right. I guessed his age in the mid-twenties. His jaw was set and his lips tight, as if in hostility and determination. I always look at a patient's fingernails because so many people with emotional problems gnaw their nails to the quick. Widdick was not a nail-biter.

"Good morning, Mr. Widdick," I said. "Please sit down."

He remained standing. His blue eyes measured me before he asked bluntly, "Who are you?"

"I'm Dr. Kleiffer."

"I thought this looked like a hospital. Tell me what I'm doing here."

Disoriented. He didn't know where he was. Patients often refuse to recognize their problems but, unless they have walled themselves off from the external world, they usually know where they are. Since I didn't know the answer to his question, I ignored it and asked, "How are you feeling?"

"Fine." Widdick sat down. "Now give me some straight answers or get me out of here. I have a wife and baby to take care of, and I'm needed at my plant." He smiled, possibly in an attempt to ingratiate himself with me. "We're doing our part to hang Kaiser Bill."

For a moment I was the one who was disoriented. Then I remembered who Kaiser Bill had been: Kaiser Wilhelm of Germany before and during World War I. At least forty years before this man across my desk could have been born. I do not believe in time travelers. If Widdick thought he was living in those days, he was severely delusional.

"Can you tell me today's date?" I asked.

"Not exactly. How long have I been here? A day? A week? It's August something, 1916."

I avoided glancing at the wall calendar for 1984 behind Widdick's back. He might turn to look, and it was too soon to confront him with reality. "What did you do here yesterday?"

"Nothing in particular."

Probably true, but the answer was an evasion. "Did you watch television?" I asked.

"What's television?"

A patient here cannot avoid television. Patients are not allowed to stay in their rooms, except for brief periods. They eat together and spend much of their time in a dayroom, where the TV set is always turned on. If Widdick couldn't remember having seen television yesterday, he suffered from loss of short-term memory. If he couldn't remember having grown up with it, he also suffered from loss of long-term memory.

I sought confirmation of short-term memory loss. "Who is your roommate?" All patients have roommates.

"Don't ask me. Do I have a roommate?"

"Yes. You are having problems with your memory, Mr. Widdick. Let's start from the beginning and establish how much you remember."

He was so precise, so positive, in what he said, and so absurd. Born March 12, 1890, in Moline, Illinois. Took a job in a steel mill in Gary, Indiana, after graduating from high school in 1898. Batted .423 for a company baseball team. Married Helen Massyk of Gary on June 25, 1913. Became a father on July 1, 1916, with the birth of a daughter, Jane. He talked warmly about Helen and proudly of Jane. "She's beginning to smile at me."

I felt sure that no historian could have tripped him up on details. A five-cent ride on a trolley car. A hand-cranked Victrola. Uneeda biscuits. Jane's birth at home with a doctor in attendance and no nurses. But nothing at all after August of 1916.

Memory begins with perception and the intellectual grasp of what is perceived. The hospital must have given Widdick batteries of tests, but I wanted to try him on one. I used several sheets of those drawings that show two or three walls of cubes from an angle. The second and third walls are hidden behind the first one except for the tops and sides of the hidden walls and the fronts of cubes exposed where cubes in front of them have been removed. One must assume the presence of hidden cubes and state the total number in the array.

Widdick got all of the totals right. Nothing was wrong with his perception or intellect.

He had concentrated visibly on the tests, lost himself in them. While I checked his answers, he leaned forward in his chair, frowned, and asked, "Who are you?"

"Dr. Kleiffer." I pressed a buzzer for an attendant to escort Widdick back to his ward.

As soon as I had seen two other patients, I went to the director's office. "Widdick appears to have Korsakov's syndrome," I told him, "but it's complicated by a delusion of a past life that he couldn't have lived. Usually a patient with Korsakov's remembers his life up to a point and then draws a blank. He doesn't invent the early part of his life and memorize details like an actor immersing himself in a role. His memory couldn't handle such a charade."

The director frowned and said, "There's more to it." He handed me a photograph. "What does this suggest to you?"

The picture looked like Widdick but older, and I said so. "It's as if his hairline had receded."

"Widdick has been here for fourteen years," the director said. "That picture was taken when he arrived."

I laughed. "Don't ask me to believe that he's growing younger."

"All I know is that he has the health and vigor of a young man and that his store of what he claims are his memories keeps dwindling farther into the past. In 1970, when he arrived, he talked about the problems of keeping his tool company alive after the crash of '29. He's forgotten about that. Did he mention his son?"

"No. Only his daughter, Jane." I looked at my notes. "Born in 1916, he said."

"He used to talk about a son, Harry, who he said was born in 1925 after his wife had two miscarriages. He hasn't mentioned Harry for years. You'll meet Harry and Jane. They say Robert Widdick has grandchildren and great-grandchildren."

"Robert Widdick! He's younger than I am." I saw a possible contradiction and asked, "How old are Harry and Jane?"

"Harry is fifty-nine and Jane is sixty-eight. That fits Widdick's story. Harry administers a trust that pays his bills."

"Do you believe that Robert Widdick is ninety-four years old?" I asked incredulously.

"I don't know what to believe. Get to know him and make up your own mind."

I must confess that Widdick's case made it hard for routine psychoses to hold my interest. Some of our patients have delusions of godhood; more often it's possession by devils. (I've never had a Napoleon.) Who seeks refuge from reality as the owner of a tool shop? I called my broker, who said there was indeed a Widdick Tool Company, very big, but it was privately held, and the assets were not made public. Perhaps Harry and Jane had concocted an elaborate fraud to gain control of the company. But thieves do not pay a hospital $12,000 a month to care for their victim. Nor can they make him appear to grow younger.

Upon reconsideration, Widdick's loss of memory did not fit Korsakov's syndrome. It is usually due to alcoholism, which causes degeneration of the mammillary bodies in the brain. Widdick was said to have been a teetotaler, and tests had shown nothing wrong with his liver or nervous system. Nor did he have a tumor or any detectable brain damage.

My meetings with Widdick always began with his asking me, "Who are you?" An hour later he would have forgotten the answer. He started every morning troubled by hospital surroundings that he didn't understand and by the feeling that his family and business needed him. Then he slipped into the hospital routine and forgot his worries. He did watch television, whether or not he understood or remembered it. He played poker, and well, for he could remember the cards for as long as it took to play a hand, and he was canny at bluffing. At our dances for patients he was a popular partner, even though he couldn't remember a woman's name five minutes after they left the floor. His feet knew what to do. The unconscious memory of procedural skills is entirely different from the memory for facts.

Donna Henlow, the recreational therapist, told me that what Widdick liked best was baseball. Patients, mostly alcoholics, fielded a team against the staff when the weather was balmy.

"He plays third base," Donna told me. "He calls it the hot corner. You should see his grin when he scoops up a hard drive! He's always talking it up, or cheering when somebody gets a hit or a score. He's really a very outgoing person when he has a chance. I wish he'd stop asking me, 'Who are you?' "

Jane and Harry Widdick arrived on the Saturday before Christmas, bearing boxes wrapped in red and green paper with red ribbons and bows. They looked their purported ages, sixty-eight and fifty-nine, if one allowed for the advantages of well-tailored clothing, exercise by Harry, and diet, a skilled hairdresser, and skin care for Jane. She had gray hair while Harry's was partly gray and thin on top.

At my request, they met me in my office after seeing Widdick alone. Jane was sniffling.

"He didn't remember me," she said. "In recent years he didn't know me and thought I was a cousin or an aunt he hadn't seen for a long time, but when I asked about his little girl he always told me how pretty she was and how much he loved her. He's forgotten. I had a bond, but it's broken."

Widdick's regression of memories has continued, I thought. Three months ago he talked of a daughter two months old. Widdick's time travels step by step with time for others, but in reverse.

"He forgot me years ago," Harry said. "It's hard to accept that empty-headed postadolescent as my father." His resentment was plain, but there was an emotional undercurrent that I couldn't identify. "Where's it going to end?" Harry asked. "You can't deny he's growing younger. I've watched it since 1950. Will he start to shrink in another ten years, revert to infancy, and die someday as an embryo without a womb?"

"Impossible," I said. Harry snorted. But he had said something I hadn't known, and I asked, "Did you say this has been going on for nearly thirty-five years?"

"Yes. It started in 1950. He was at the office and saw a big order for machine tools and raised hell because no one had told him about it. Well, he had clinched the sale himself, the previous day. I was working as his assistant, and I persuaded him to see a doctor, who said he had amnesia but couldn't find a cause. Next day he asked the doctor, 'Who are you?' The amnesia spread through his brain like cancer."

"I have three children," Jane said. "Dad forgot them one by one. Harry's two boys were born in the mid-fifties. Mother told him and told him about them but he couldn't remember for more than an hour. He's never known that he has seven great-grandchildren. He was proud of his family, proud of Harry's service as a sailor late in the war, proud of putting us through college and seeing us marry. Now the last shred of that is gone."

"It's tragic to build a good life and lose all knowledge of it," I said. "But the burden of handling his affairs and caring for him fell on you. How did you cope?"

"Dad reorganized the company as a corporation after the war and gave stock to Mother and us, but he kept a majority interest," Harry said. "We had to go to court and put his share into trust, with Mother as trustee. I'm trustee now. If Dad ever comes back to normal he'll own a bigger company and have a lot more money than he left behind." He snorted again. "Fat chance."

I was more interested in what Jane said.

"Dad stayed at home for twenty years." Jane shook her head at the memory. "In 1950 he was sixty years old, and Mother was fifty-six. They had servants, and she could handle him without trouble except early in the morning when he wanted to go to the office and she had to persuade him to take the day off. One day he went for a walk and forgot where he lived. He took a taxi to the house he had lived in before and got into a furious argument with the woman he found there. She called the police, who called Harry, who straightened it out. After that Mother couldn't let him go for walks alone. He was all right at home, even if he couldn't remember where the rooms were. He was even handy around the house, fixing things like the washing machine and the lawn mower. Dad's a mechanical genius. But he began to doubt that Mother was his wife. He grew younger while she grew older, you see."

"Mother couldn't take it," Harry said.

"No," Jane agreed. "In 1970 he was talking about things that happened in 1930, when he was forty years old, and that's the age he looked, but Mother was seventy-six. He thought she was her own mother and kept asking, 'Where's Helen?' A wife can accept her lot if she has to care for an eighty-year-old husband who's feeble, but a husband who's younger than their own son and ignores her? I think bitterness is what killed her. That's when we brought him here."

We were silent while I tried to imagine twenty years of details, so many of them wearisome from repetition, and their growing feeling of helplessness and abandonment of hope for Robert Widdick. And growing hostility toward a man who grew ever younger while they aged.

"He's a freak!" Jane burst out. "I can't love him anymore. He's a monster."

"I'll tell you what bothers me," Harry said. "Dad was sixty when this happened to him. I'll be sixty next May. Could whatever ails him be inherited?"

"I don't know." The possibility hadn't occurred to me. "It's brand-new. The loss of memory could be caused by a degenerative disease that damages the brain cells. If so, it might be inherited. I'll look into it."

By now I was convinced that Robert Widdick was ninety-four years old but looked twenty-six, going on twenty-five. Of what value was youth without the ability to learn and remember? The loss of memory mattered, not the appearance of rejuvenation. I arranged to have a geneticist I knew, a woman who was doing research into abnormalities of chromosomes, take a look at the nuclei of cells extracted from the growth layer of Widdick's skin.

Early in January of 1985 my friend called me. "This is fantastic!" she exclaimed. "Do you know what a man's sex chromosomes look like?"

Yes, I knew. Chromosomes can be identified when they condense during mitosis before replication for cell division. Twenty-two pairs of chromosomes in every cell have members of equal length. So do a woman's sex chromosomes, in every cell, but not a man's. His X-chromosome, from his mother, is of medium length, but the Y-chromosome, from his father, is short.

"The short arm of a man's Y-chromosome ends close to the centromere," she said. "This guy's Y has extra DNA at the tip of the short arm. A stain for banding shows it. It's probably a single gene. Tell me about him."

"He's a patient who suffers from both short-term and long-term memory loss." I didn't tell her about the reversal of age. "We may be looking at a problem that's genetic in origin. If so, I suppose it could be inherited."

"You bet it could, but only by males, who get the Y-chromosome from their fathers. Females don't have a Y. And it takes only one freak chromosome to cause the body to go haywire."

I felt obligated to inform Harry Widdick that his father's problems could be genetic. "That's guesswork, but an educated guess. If you have inherited the potentiality for the syndrome, I'm afraid I can't offer any comfort. All you can do is prepare for it to hit you." I didn't tell him that his sons and their sons could also be affected.

But I thought about that and about the growing number of men in succeeding generations who would lose their memories and grow younger. Until what? Would Robert Widdick stop growing whiskers and shrink, as Harry had put it?

The change, in March, was more remarkable, completely unexpected. Donna Henlow ran into my office, pushing her way past a patient who was waiting. "He called me Donna!" she exclaimed. "He knew me! I went to remind him of a Ping-Pong tournament, and he knew me!"

Never mind the waiting patient, who wanted to tell me that everybody hated him. Of course they did, and would until he stopped pestering them for reassurance. I had to see Widdick. A spontaneous remission after thirty-five years? I was as excited as Donna.

As she followed me, I found Widdick in the hall on his way to my office. "Dr. Kleiffer!" he said. So he remembered me, too. "Something very strange is happening. Yesterday you were talking to me about my memory. I didn't understand the problem but I began to notice things. I watched a nurse make a phone call by pushing buttons! I never saw a telephone like that before. I didn't say anything. Then Donna asked me if I'd like a cup of coffee. She called me Bob, but I had to ask who she was. Obviously there was something wrong with my memory." Widdick grinned at her. "I'm not a man to forget pretty girls."

Smiling, she brushed her blond hair back with one hand.

But Widdick was too full of discoveries to dally upon gallantry. "The coffee came from a machine that works with coins. Great idea. Why hadn't I heard of it? But fifty cents a cup? That's piracy. Then I watched television. I've seen movies but they didn't have sound and color. Did they have a projector in that little box? My roommate told me they broadcast it like radio. And the things it showed! Airplanes without propellers! After supper they had a news broadcast with pictures of a president I never heard of."

"Wonderful!" Donna exclaimed. She grabbed him, kissed him on the cheek, and fled down the hallway.

Widdick followed her with his eyes and smiled. "I'm a married man. When will I see my wife? She's pregnant, you know."

"Let's go into my office." The patient was still waiting, and I sent him away. Not therapeutic. Proof to him that I hated him. So what? Patients are endlessly resourceful in finding nails to pound into the coffins around their minds. Widdick had remembered Donna's name and mine. He knew where to find me. He had recovered his short-term memory—if it lasted. Long-term memory was apparently still gone. I had to find out.

When we were seated, I asked Widdick what year it was.

"Look, after what I saw on television I'm not going to guess how many years I've forgotten.

What I remember is 1915, but that's not right, is
it?"

I asked him to look at the wall calendar. "It's
1985."

"Nonsense. You can't tell me I'm ninety-five
years old." He got out of his chair, grasped one leg
of it with one hand, and lifted the chair, holding it
level, as high as his shoulder. "Could a ninety-five-
year-old man do that?"

"I couldn't do it myself," I said. "What's impossible, but seems to be true, is that you've been growing younger since you reached the age of sixty."

Nobody could be expected to adjust to a statement
like that immediately. Widdick sat down slowly,
stared at me, clasped his hands, and stared at them.
"What's happened to my wife?" he asked softly.

"She died. I'm sorry."

"Helen can't be dead!" he protested. "She's only
twenty-one. I love her!"

"She died in 1970 at the age of seventy-six," I
told him quietly. "She left you a daughter and a
son. You also have five grandchildren and seven
great-grandchildren."

"Who cares about them? I don't know them."

"You cared once," I said, foreseeing trouble.
"Your son and daughter have been taking care of
you here. You'll meet them."

But not yet. I had to be confident that he had
recovered the ability to remember new things before
I called Jane and Harry. Widdick should have a
chance to become oriented to seventy years of
change. Donna took care of a lot of that. She devoted
so much time to Widdick that the director called her
in for a stern reminder not to neglect other patients.

"He's very quick," Donna told me. "After all, he

knows machinery and electricity. He had me get him some books about computers."

After I told Harry and Jane that their father appeared to be making a remarkable recovery, they met him in my office, at my request, so that I could observe the reactions. At first all three were stiff and hesitant, strangers with an implausible bond. Harry and Jane had come to resent their father's interminable illness and, no doubt, the money it cost. He resented having two senior citizens foisted upon him as his offspring.

"I appreciate all you've done for me," Widdick said at last. "You have to understand that it will take me a while to get used to you as my children."

"Because of our age?" Jane asked crossly. "How do you think I feel about a father who's younger than my son?"

"Tell me about the children and grandchildren," he said. Jane calmed down, and I realized that Widdick had started his career as a man who had a gift for handling people as well as machines. He would need that skill, it appeared, after he got Harry to talk about the tool company. "And you've been running it since you were twenty-five," Widdick said. Then, casually, "That seems to be my age now. I won't be here much longer. Should I get back on the job?"

Harry, who felt threatened, loosed a volley of objections. "The company has grown. I thought I made that clear. You're a million years behind the times. Changes in production and distribution are only the start of it. Tax laws have changed. We're dealing with a union. We're swamped in government regulations. I'll find a good job for you while you learn the ropes."

Aha! I thought. The age-old Oedipal conflict between father and son takes a new twist. But which one of them is Oedipus and which the king?

Widdick thought in more straightforward terms, I discovered after his children left. "That man thinks he can steal my company," he said. "Not after I get my stock out of trust."

His unexpected rapacity irritated me until I realized that Widdick did not remember Harry or what Harry had done for him. "How are you going to prove you are Robert Widdick, born in 1890?" I asked him. "What will you answer when Harry tells a judge you've been out of your mind for thirty-five years?"

"After seeing me regularly all these years, my dear son will establish my identity," he said with a grin, "and I'm not out of my mind now. The problem will be explaining my youthful appearance when I'm ninety-five years old. I'll think of something."

My only clue about what he had in mind was his persistent questioning about what had happened to him. I explained chromosomes, which he knew nothing about, and described the extra gene on his Y-chromosomes, in every cell, that could be at the root of his rejuvenation and loss of memory, although I didn't know how. His mind leaped quickly from knowledge that the Y was inherited only and always by sons to the strong probability that all of his male descendants, not only Harry but Harry's sons and grandsons, would be trapped in turn in a reversal of aging.

"We're all in the same boat. That will take some thought."

He was patient, content to let Harry stew while

he stayed in the hospital, except for excursions with Donna or Jane to complete his grasp of change. Perhaps I should have foreseen the next surprise.

Irrepressible Donna couldn't conceal her news. "Bob asked me to marry him!" she told me happily.

"Robert Widdick?" Of course, she said. I got her out of the clouds and into a chair and asked, "What if this happens to him again?"

"But it couldn't!" she protested.

"It shouldn't have happened the first time." I told her about Widdick's aberrant Y-chromosomes. "Genes have to be triggered to work their physiological magic. What if the environment of an aging body is what triggers Widdick's genes? What if it's something like the onset of cancer? Widdick's fancy genes rush to the defense, and they overreact. They take him back to an age of full vigor, but at the cost of wiping out his memories to create a younger brain."

"Oh," Donna said. Then, defiantly, "We'll have thirty-five good years together. He's getting a second chance."

Her lack of understanding depressed me. I shook my head and said, "He starts with the same formative years. He has no memory of what he did right or wrong after he was twenty-five, no chance to second-guess himself, none of the benefits of hindsight. It's not a second chance but another first chance. Maybe not as good a one. He faces a lot of hostility in his family."

And possibly from the public, I thought.

"We'll manage," Donna said firmly. "But . . . could this happen again and again? Could Bob be immortal?"

"Not really. Maybe it will happen again and

maybe it won't, but people die of a lot of things besides old age. Sooner or later an accident would catch him."

Donna was subdued when she left, but I had no doubt that she would marry Widdick. I wondered whether he would go through his seventy-year cycle again, thirty-five years of active life followed by thirty-five years of being drained by the struggle of his genes for immortality. Starting each cycle in 1915. Widdick could grasp the changes of seventy years, but twice seventy? Three times seventy? He would buy one life at the cost of another, never knowing what he had lost. Life is not a string, measured by its length. Life is a tapestry, woven well or badly but not meant to be unraveled.

The director agreed that there was no medical reason to keep Widdick in the hospital. Harry told me over the phone, without enthusiasm, that he and Jane would pick him up. They found Donna in my office with Widdick and me.

"I want you to meet Donna Henlow," he told them. "Donna has consented to be my wife."

Jane stiffened as if frozen upright in her chair. Harry offered his hand to Donna, said, "Glad to meet you," and walked over to stare out a window. Jane recovered her poise and said, "Forgive me for being taken aback. I was thinking of Mother, but that's past history. I must congratulate Father." Harry continued to stare out the window, and Donna looked offended.

Harry took a deep breath and turned to us. He stared at Donna.

"I haven't had the pleasure of meeting this charming young lady," Harry said. "Who are you?"

Chapter Two

We are fortunate that Robert, foreseeing his needs, wrote out what he did, why he did it, and how he felt. Keeping diaries became common among single-f's, and many of these tell about Robert, but his own words remain the best source for understanding him. This early letter reveals the imagination, the diplomacy and forcefulness, and sometimes the lies with which he sought survival of himself and his family. It also contains our first account of Rosalind and Richard, the saint and sinner of our early annals.

—GABRIEL (D) CHEN, ARCHIVIST

Letter from Robert Widdick to Himself (2022)

It must have happened again, or you wouldn't be reading this. I am you.

Up to a point. We are the same man for our first twenty-five years. For the next thirty-five we lead different lives. Then it's like diving into the Fountain of Youth and hitting your head on a rock. The memory of those thirty-five years is drained out of you as you spend another thirty-five gaining strength to climb back on dry land.

Time comes unglued for us. You know you were born in 1890. You thought it was now 1915 and you were twenty-five years old, but they have told you at the hospital that it's the year 2055, which makes you 165. Not really. One hundred forty of those years have been erased. You are twenty-five again.

The same thing happens to our male descendants. Life is dangerous for us because people fear and hate freaks, which is what we are. Genetic freaks. (You will have to learn genetics all over again.) As I write this letter in the year 2020 there are fourteen of us.

And you are me. If you don't believe that, I will tell you something I wouldn't know unless we were the same person. When I was ten years old I stole a handful of licorice whips from a bin in a grocery store. I ran home and hid behind the house and ate them all, knowing that what I had done was wrong. We know ourselves by secret guilt.

Your doctor must have explained the R-factor to you. That's what we call the extra gene on our Y-chromosomes. R stands for regression, reversion, reversal, rejuvenation, recycling. We enter the R-Phase when we blank out and grow younger. When we come out of it we enter the N-Phase, N for new. The cost is our memory since the first time we became twenty-five. You won't like having paid that bill.

Forgetfulness is a frightful curse. "Forgetfulness is a form of death," Dr. Kleiffer told me. He's dead now. You have forgotten him, so part of you has also died.

For thirty-five years I have kept a diary to remind myself, meaning you, of what I will have forgotten. This is just an introduction. The printouts will reveal ghosts of your life and help you get things straight, starting with the names of your descendants. There will be more of them in 2055, of course, than those I knew. In 2020, as I write, I have thirteen male descendants with the R-factor. I can't keep track of all of the daughters and granddaughters and their sons, none of whom possess our mocking simulacrum of immortality.

Two of your grandsons, Jim and Bill, were in the hospital when you entered it for your second R-Phase. They remembered you, but as a much younger man, and as they grew younger themselves, they forgot. You must have been furious when they failed to recognize you any longer. More recently three of your great-grandsons must have entered the hospital. You will have remembered them as younger than they looked. There must have been many times when you didn't know what they were talking about.

Six years before 2055 your second son, Dick, should have entered the R-Phase. So far it always hits us at sixty years old, and he was born in 1989. You will meet him again. Watch out for him.

When you came out of the R-Phase this time you remembered marrying Helen in 1913 and founding the tool company two years later just before she became pregnant. Once again you were deeply in love with her and were shattered when they told you she had died long ago. The pregnancy ended with the birth of your first daughter, Jane. She lived to be eighty-six and was a great help to me.

Helen also had a son, Harry, who has the R-factor. He did a good job running the tool company while I was a blank. But he entered the R-Phase as I came out of it, and I can only hope that someday there is a variation in the length of our cycles that lets them overlap so that I can get to know him.

In 1985, after the beginning of my second N-Phase, I married Donna Henlow. If I could give you only one piece of advice, it would be this: Don't be in a hurry to marry again. Your love for Helen will punish you if you do. So may your wife, as Donna did me.

While our marriage was going smoothly, we had two children, Rosalind and Richard. Dick was always a misfit and now threatens us all. But Roz! For the thirty-three years of her life so far I have lived with the bitter knowledge that someday I will forget what a delight she is.

How do you get started on a second life as a young man? Donna, who was recreation therapist at the hospital, took an enthusiastic interest in my recovery and helped me catch up with change. A lot of things, like frozen foods, refrigerators instead of iceboxes, and milk that came in cartons were new but not revolutionary. Computers and DNA genetics were. Fortunately I had worked with electric relays and I knew about animal breeding, so I was not in a complete fog when I had to learn about what was new. I saw at once that computers had brought a radical change to business methods. Genetics promised to affect our lives even more.

My first daughter, Jane, who was now 69, often claimed me to herself. She brought scrapbooks and photograph albums. Cued by what I saw in these, I could say things like, "That was when I taught you to ride a bicycle." A well-aimed remark set her off like a string of firecrackers in memories that she thought I shared. "You were a pretty girl from the day you were born," I would say while she rattled on. Or "I used to like to have you sit on my lap." Convinced that I loved her as much as ever, she forgot that I looked younger than her children.

It was all an act. I remembered nothing. I tried, but I couldn't. I tried because I hoped to find something I had lost, a love of Jane that had obviously been precious to me, and because I felt that a father owed no less to his daughter, but I could not love faded snapshots or clippings yellowed by age.

I confess that I had another motive. With Harry in the hospital, Jane had succeeded him as trustee of my assets, and I wanted to regain control without fuss. What I wanted to do would take lots of money.

Jane invited me to move in with her and her husband until I married Donna, but I declined and rented an apartment. Jane's husband took me for some kind of cousin, which was the pose I adopted, with Jane's connivance.

Handling my son Harry's family was tricky. Dr. Kleiffer felt obliged to tell his wife what was happening to him. A wife often goes into a tailspin when her husband dies; Harry's outlandish way of abandoning her was worse. She didn't want to believe it. She had never come to the hospital with Harry to see me, so Kleiffer asked me to join her and Harry in his office to show her that Harry, in time, would make an astonishing recovery.

"Mrs. Widdick," Kleiffer said, "this is Robert Widdick, your husband's father. He had your husband's problem but has come out of it."

She stared at me with surprise, confusion, and immediate disbelief. "How dare you say such a thing!" she exclaimed to Kleiffer. "Robert Widdick is a very old man, and he's been sick for years." She turned back to me. "You're an imposter. You're after the money in Robert Widdick's trust."

Obviously Harry had never told her about the strange changes in me, the skeleton in the family closet. "Ask Harry," I said. "He watched me grow younger."

Harry had entered the R-Phase so recently that he remembered my recovery as well as my years in the hospital. "It's true," he said.

"I don't believe you," she told him. She was as thin as a wasp and as ready to sting. "You can't even remember what happened last week."

"Dr. Kleiffer can show you pictures the hospital took of me from the time I came here until I was discharged as a young man," I told her. "If Harry follows the same course, which he should, he will become twenty-five again."

"While I grow old and die. Do you think that's a comfort?"

"No. But Harry is fond of you and wants you to be comfortable and as happy as possible. If there's anything I can do, I will."

"I'll depend on myself and my children, thank you. You're a swindler. You belong in jail. I know why Harry is backing your story. This doctor here hypnotized him."

"Hypnotism would be unethical," Kleiffer protested, as if no one could question a doctor's ethics. "I can think of nothing to gain by it and a lot to lose. What we have here is a syndrome of overwhelming medical interest, and we must study it."

"Just you, I hope," I said in sudden alarm.

"I'm the only one at the hospital who knows about the R-factor. Obviously that's the way you want it. I do hope, Mrs. Widdick, that you will keep this to yourself."

She looked at him with a tight smile. "I've got you over a barrel, have I? You and your syndrome! We'll see. How about my children. Aren't they supposed to know about their own father?"

Jane had told me about Harry's two sons, James and William, and about five grandchildren, three boys and two girls. "Of course they should know," I said. "If I can convince Jim and Bill that a young man like me is their grandfather, maybe you'll be satisfied."

"You'll find out they're too smart for you."

In 1985 Jim was thirty-five and a lawyer. Bill was thirty-two and worked for Widdick Tool Co. as assistant manager of one of our four plants. I had built the first three but remembered only the first one. Harry had built the fourth after I entered the R-Phase. I couldn't help comparing my education, which ended with high school, with that of my grandsons. Jim had a B.A. in history and a law degree. Bill had his bachelor's in engineering and a master's from business school. What they had missed was my training in the famous school of hard knocks.

I persuaded Jane to ask them to meet her in Kleiffer's office after one of their visits to the hospital to see their father. I waited in another room while Kleiffer and Jane told them about Harry and me and the R-factor. Kleiffer came for me and said, "I think they have accepted the situation. Meeting you will be a shock, of course."

They watched me enter the office as nervously as if I had been a leopard stalking them. Jane saw their reaction and smiled. I smiled, too, and said, "I suggest you call me Bob. None of us would be comfortable with Grandpa."

Jim shook his head and said, "I'd hate to try and sell a jury on this. You're so young!"

"You'll be in the same boat someday. Did Dr. Kleiffer explain that?"

Both of them snapped their heads toward Kleiffer so fast that I knew he hadn't told them the whole story. "I assumed that you would understand that," he said. "I explained the R-factor on the Y-chromosomes. You inherited your Ys from Harry just as he inherited his from Robert."

"We'd better be sure," Jim said. "You haven't checked our chromosomes, doctor."

"That's hardly necessary."

"When I build a case in court, I can't rely on assumptions, even if they're logical. Can you test us?"

"As far as that goes, I can't prove that the R-factor caused what happened to Robert and Harry or that the same thing will happen to you, although I see no other explanation and no other result." Kleiffer sounded offended that his judgment had been questioned. "I'll have somebody take tissue samples for tests."

He made a phone call. While we waited, Bill asked me, "Do you feel as young as you look?"

"Mostly. I have the strength and energy of a young man. My hair has grown back. There's just one thing." I grinned and pulled a surprise. I took out my false teeth, a partial upper plate, and laid them on the table. "We don't grow young enough to reach the age at which teeth are formed. These are hardware."

Jane hadn't known that. She looked startled and uncomfortable and said, "Please! Put them back." I did so.

A young resident fresh from his internship came in with some kind of punch to take samples down through the skin, dropped the samples in bottles, and labeled the bottles. Eventually the samples showed that both of them had the R-factor.

"I suppose you've given some thought to how we should all handle this," Jim said.

I certainly had. "It comes down to survival. First, we should keep this as quiet as we can. People would call us freaks, and people don't like freaks. Agreed?"

They nodded their heads. Jane frowned, so I said, "Jane is an exception. She understands." Let her enjoy being part of a conspiracy of silence. "Your wives and children are entitled to know. The question is when, and how much." Jim had two sons, aged twelve and ten, and a girl, seven. Bill had a boy, four, and a girl, two. "I suggest holding off on the daughters as long as possible, maybe until you're about to enter the R-Phase yourselves.

Bring your wives in from time to time to see what's happening to your father. Tell the women about the amnesia but not about the chance for a second life. The sons should know the full story earlier so they can make plans. Maybe when they're about twenty-five. That will be up to you."

"Not until after they're married, or they would be bound to warn their prospective brides what they were in for," Bill said.

"They shouldn't be unfair," Jim objected.

I liked Jim for that, but how could you tell a girl you were a freak and expect her to march happily to the altar? "You have a long time to think it over," I said. "What we must start preparing for now are the years when more and more of us will be in the R-Phase at the same time. Do you realize that a couple of your boys will be in the R-Phase before you come out of it? I'll be there ahead of them. That's five at once. The number will multiply with every generation."

"Good Lord!" Jim whispered.

"But . . ." Kleiffer began. He frowned. "Look. You can't have two or more men from the same family in a hospital together showing the same very unusual symptoms without having doctors know there's a genetic problem."

I was ready for him. "One doctor who can be trusted is all we need. Nurses and aides can be changed before they realize that Harry is growing younger. Meanwhile, waiting for the crowd to arrive, we see to it that some of our children and grandchildren become doctors so we have a steady supply from our own family."

"Are you talking about a private hospital for the Widdick family?" Kleiffer asked.

I wondered whether there would ever be so many of us that we needed our own hospital. Not for a long time, so I shook my head. "We should be hidden among patients who have amnesia for other reasons. Other kinds of patients, too."

I explained my plan. The Widdick Tool Co. earned roughly forty million dollars a year. My trust owned a majority of the stock, and Harry and Jane owned the rest. The stock would be given to a charitable foundation. Call it the Health Research Foundation, nothing too specific. The foundation would build a hospital and meet deficits with income from the company. The hospital would support research into genetics and the workings of the brain as well as areas that had nothing to do with the Widdicks. Directors of the foundation would be a self-perpetuating board composed solely of members of the family. Let the tool company operate as a subsidiary whose officers would be picked by the foundation board.

"You could draw up the papers, couldn't you, Jim?" I asked.

"Hold on!" Bill interrupted. "Jim and I stand to inherit our father's stock. That's worth a lot of money. Why should we let it go to your foundation?"

"You forget that Harry won't die and you forget that it's your foundation, too. It will take care of you in the future, no one knows how many times, and it will take care of all of your descendants who inherit the R-factor."

"What about our wives and daughters?" Jim asked.

"We figure out a pension scheme for them and see to it that you make enough to give them a good income after you phase out."

"Mother will never stand for giving away Dad's stock," Bill said.

Probably true. She detested me and the whole weird situation. "All right. The tool company can borrow money to buy Harry's stock. When the tool company turns its assets over to the foundation, we pay the loan back with the borrowed money. Does your mother control the stock?"

"No," Jim answered. "No trust for him has been set up yet."

"When one is, see that you and Bill are trustees. Do what you want to with his other assets but save the stock for the foundation. We'll buy yours, too, Jane. And I will ask you to give all the stock in my trust to the foundation, not to me. Will you do that for me?"

"I guess so," she said after hesitating, "but how will you earn a living?"

"I will pay myself a good salary as foundation president."

"You have big ideas for a man of twenty-five, which you're supposed to be now," Bill said. "Do you plan to take over the company, too?"

He's afraid that I'll get in the way of his ambitions, I thought as I answered. "Not for a long time, if ever. I know how to run a lathe, but I don't know anything about computerized robot-controlled assembly lines, which the company uses now." Jane had given me annual reports to read. "I'll be busy with the foundation. I'll depend on you to tell me what I need to know about the business. Who's running it now?"

"The vice president, now that Dad is in the hospital."

"Make him president, if you thinks he's up to

it. You take over when you're ready."

Bill subsided into silence. I turned to Kleiffer. "You're a key man in all of this, doctor. I hope you will consent to become director of our hospital. You pick the research projects and hire the staff. All I ask in return is that you handle any Widdicks who come along personally."

This was shiny bait wriggling on the hook for a man of thirty-six, which I knew he was. I was surprised that he hesitated. "I like a general practice of psychiatry," he said slowly. "I don't know whether I'd be any good at administration."

"You could hire someone for that," I answered. "You could work with psychiatric patients as you chose. Meanwhile you would build a research facility to rival the best university hospitals, and you would be responsible for getting a tremendous amount of valuable work done." Having offered as much temptation, for a man of his dedication, as the devil at his best, I casually made a threat. "It's the only way I can see for you to continue your study of"—I almost said, "our peculiarities," but I had learned a better word from him—"our syndrome."

"I'll give it a try," he said without enthusiasm.

"Let's get back to you," Jim said to me. "Are you supposed to remain Robert Widdick, age ninety-five? You've been collecting Social Security and Medicare for years. If that goes on and on, you'll blow the computers."

Definitely, I liked Jim. "We'll file a death certificate for me." Kleiffer looked alarmed, so I said, "I won't ask you to perjure yourself, doctor. I had to deal with some rough people when I got started, and I know how to find a doctor drowning in alcohol who will be happy to fill out a death certificate for a few bucks. Then fake a cremation. It will be fun to read my own obituary. I won't forge a new birth certificate. I will be Robert Widdick, born in 1960 in some town where the courthouse burned down with all its records. A distant cousin. I'll grow a beard. It won't be hard to get a new Social Security card and driver's license and credit cards."

Kleiffer appeared ready to go into shock, but Jim acted as if he were cross-examining a witness. "Old pictures?" he asked. "School records? Military service?"

"I wasn't old enough to serve in any wars. I lost my scrap albums. I didn't show up for a picture in the high school annual. I never went to college. And I'll keep my head down to avoid questions."

"Do we have to do the same thing for Dad and us?" Bill asked.

"It looks that way. We can make it better by changing names for each N-Phase so too many Widdicks don't parade in front of the public. We'll keep track of who they are."

"Let's kick that around," Jim said. "In 1985 I am thirty-five years old. Assume that I enter the R-Phase in 2010 and come out of it in 2045 at the apparent age of twenty-five and supposedly born in 2020. I can pick a new name for myself in advance. The foundation can register a birth for me in 2020 and go on from there. The idea presents some interesting problems."

Jim and Bill not only resembled me, a little taller but with similar square faces and the same brown hair, but they shared my unwillingness to waste time disputing facts and my taste for devious planning.

I left in high spirits and took Donna to dinner.

I saw no reason to delay our marriage further, and she agreed happily to have it soon.

I'm not sure why I married Donna. She was lively and good-looking, she had helped me recover from grief over the death of Helen, she had taken an enthusiastic part in my recovery, and she was affectionate. Caught on the rebound, I thought that I loved her. Perhaps I was an easy victim of flirtation. Perhaps I felt a need to restore the warmth of family life that I had lost. Perhaps I had a subconscious desire to increase the number of Widdicks in the world, for there is strength in numbers.

We were too different. When, as my wife, Donna no longer had to work for a living, she lost interest in the painting and exercise classes and other activities she had organized for patients at the hospital. Many patients were apathetic, mired in private worlds of delusion, and I didn't blame her for quitting. But she had no other strong interests. She dabbled in charities as a volunteer, shopped for things she didn't need, and watched a lot of television. We both enjoyed parties, but I was interested in other people, with always at the back of my mind the thought of how different they were from me. All Donna wanted was entertainment.

What it boils down to is that she was superficial. While I slaved to organize the foundation and help Kleiffer build a research hospital from scratch, her interest was perfunctory. While I, as president of the foundation that owned the Widdick companies, played an ever greater part in company affairs, she was satisfied with my paycheck.

I persuaded Jim and Bill to change the name of the company to New World Technology and buy a small biogenetics firm. It would help support foundation research in exchange for patents. Donna didn't realize that I had acted to remove the Widdick name from public exposure and had added a branch that might bring large profits.

How different it had been with Helen! She had worked with me in the office while I had been starting Widdick Tool Co. Our projects were joint projects. Donna was never a partner. I could not forget those bright early years, which seemed so recent, with Helen.

Cracks in my marriage to Donna appeared with the birth of Rosalind early in 1987. "That damn kid!" Donna would exclaim when the baby cried to waken her for feedings at night. I would take Roz to her and then back to her crib, and I would think of how angelically she slept after she was fed and changed. I watched every new wiggle that Roz made as she grew, and I cheered her first smile. "I think you love her more than you do me," Donna said. My heart sank at this ominous sign of rivalry between mother and daughter.

Dick, who was born in 1989, caused less trouble at night but he brought dissension, too. He looked like a baby, no more or less, to me, but Donna insisted that he looked like my side of the family. "I've brought another freak into the world," she said.

This made me angry. "You were happy to marry one," I said sharply.

Donna retreated. She smiled and answered, "I'm glad I did. Dick will be fine."

The bust-up came during a period of wild inflation, which brought price controls and rationing of raw materials. Bill had become president of New World Enterprises, but I was the one who knew how to deal with a black market. One night I came home tired after figuring out a new way to hide payments under the table. I lay with Donna in my arms and said, "I don't think I could keep going without you, Helen."

Donna pushed away from me and jumped out of bed. She yelled at me. "I'm Donna! You'd better learn my name!"

"I'm sorry, Donna. It was just a slip."

"It's what you've been hiding all this time, isn't it. You're still in love with Helen!"

I reached out for her with my arms and said, "That's silly. Don't make a big thing out of a small mistake."

"It's not small to me! You and your freak memory! You want to live with a ghost! I'm real but you don't care." She started to cry and left to spend the night in the guest room.

I didn't follow her. There was too much truth in what she had said.

Next morning she said nothing at breakfast, not even "Good morning," and she turned her head aside when I tried to kiss her good-bye for the day. When I returned that evening I found the papers in my desk disarranged. She had rifled the drawers, taken my few old pictures of Helen, and tossed them out with the garbage.

I retrieved the pictures, spotted and smelly, and waved them in Donna's face. "That was vicious!" I said. "You're crazy with jealousy. Helen was part of my life, too. Are you trying to destroy my life?"

"You're living a new life now. I'm helping you shake off the mud of an old life."

Her malicious pretense that she was being helpful infuriated me. "You want a life that suits only you.

I want a life that suits me. If you fit into it, fine; if not, get out!"

Naturally a divorce followed soon. We agreed to have the children stay with us by turns, and I bought another house. Donna tried to turn both children against me. There were bad moments.

Once when Roz was eleven years old she came to my house, dodged aside when I tried to welcome her with a kiss, and burst into tears as she ran to her room. I waited ten minutes before knocking on her door. "Come in," she said in a low voice. She was sitting on the edge of her bed, and she stared at me with a face twisted with accusation and pain.

"Mom says I'll grow old and die but you'll grow younger and live forever," Roz said. "She says you're a monster who ought to live in a zoo or in a lab where scientists could study you like a rat. She says you'll forget all about me, like I was somebody in ancient history."

This was the day I had dreaded, the inevitable day of revelation. I hoped that Roz felt secure in my love for her. "I won't live forever," I said. Then I told the necessary lie, not the truth that tormented me. "And I won't forget you."

Her face brightened, and I knew that the fear of being forgotten was what had troubled her. "Will you grow younger?" she asked.

"Probably, someday, but not for many years yet."

"Mom says when you grow younger you forget everything back to the time when you were twenty-five years old. She says that was a hundred years ago. Are you really that old?"

"Not really. All but twenty-five years were erased and don't count, so I'm really thirty-eight."

Suddenly she was suspicious again. "How come

you won't forget me when you're erased next time?"

"Because I have a lot of tapes of you." Not that those would restore gut feelings, as I knew from experience with my first daughter, Jane. "Besides, after I'm younger I'll see you again."

"But I'll be older than you. How will you know me?"

"You'll still be you."

She hesitated, trying to imagine a reversal of relative ages. "When you grow younger it must be like you were going somewhere and met yourself coming back."

This is a bright girl, I thought. "Something like that, except that you don't know it's happening."

"Where will it happen?"

"In a hospital." She didn't know that Harry was in the hospital. We don't talk about Harry.

"I'll take care of you until you come out and see me again."

This time my eyes held the tears. This time she accepted my kiss.

Knowing what had happened to me, Roz was fascinated with genetics. By the time she entered high school she knew more about chromosomes than they taught in biology class. "They tie all kinds of life together!" she reported enthusiastically. Grinning, she added, "And they're cute little wiggly things."

My son—your son—Dick had problems that I couldn't solve. He was handsome, blond like his mother, and attracted girls, but usually not for long because he was self-centered and moody. He spoke forcefully, often abrasively, and with no more wit than a codfish. And he refused to take his studies seriously. When I asked him about school, he answered contemptuously, "That junk!"

Since he got good grades, he could argue that he didn't need to study. I came to realize that he had a phenomenal memory. He could pass a test easily if all he had to do was parrot what he had heard in class. In math he could reach many answers intuitively without proceeding from A through B and C to D. He was not learning to reason, to solve problems systematically, to marshal facts and weigh options.

"You have a good mind," I told him. "Don't let it rust. It's like baseball. If you don't go to batting practice, you can't hit a pitch in a game."

The analogy did as much good as cough medicine on a fractured skull. "Junk," he repeated, and turned away.

Once he told me, "Mom says you're a freak who lives over and over again."

"No one can be sure of that, but if I'm a freak, so are you. Did she tell you that?"

"Yes. I don't want to be a freak."

"We're not freaks. We're different, that's all. Maybe it's a good thing."

"It's wrong. It's bad."

In high school he took up holographic art and at the same time joined the Church of Divine Prophecy. When he wasn't memorizing the Book of Revelation, he designed scenes of Hell on his computer. He portrayed the damned with bodies contorted and faces twisted in pain as they burned in the heart of nuclear explosions.

One evening be brought me a Bible with a passage from Psalm 90 underlined and asked, "Have you read this?"

The text read: "The days of our years are three score and ten, and if in our strength they be four score years, yet their strength is labor and sorrow, for it is soon cut off and we fly away."

"I've read it."

"We aren't supposed to live more than eighty years," Dick said. His lips were tight, and he stared at me as if he had caught me stealing treasure from a vault.

"That's a report on what usually happens, not a commandment. A lot of people live more than eighty years."

"It says what is right. It's a sin to live longer. You're a sinner, and I will be, too, if I grow younger someday. We'll be punished in Hell for it."

"Not if we make good use of our lives. Think of the extra good you can do."

"I can preach the truth," he said.

Apparently some feelings were stronger than a sense of sin. When Dick was a junior in high school he made a girl pregnant. She came to me to ask me to persuade him to marry her. I tried, but he refused. At his age, seventeen, marriage would have been impractical, but he had a different reason for refusal. He argued that she should be punished for tempting him.

At that time it was customary to study cells from the chorionic villae of a fetus after eight weeks of pregnancy to detect abnormal chromosomes in time for an easy abortion. Dr. Kleiffer studied the cells, which had the same genetic makeup as the fetus, and reported that the baby would be a boy, with the R-factor. Wanting the factor to spread, I paid the girl to have the baby and promised support. Several years later she married a man named Broadmead, who adopted the child. So now there's a Philip Broadmead and his male line for us to include among the Widdicks.

Dick entered a Bible college but was caught in the draft for the Food Wars. World population had reached 7.7 billion, and millions of people starved every year. Hordes of desperate men streamed from the Middle East toward the Ukraine, from Africa into France, and from Latin American countries into the United States. Before they were driven back, Dick's left arm was shredded by shrapnel in the Battle of Riverside. A surgeon cut it off. I doubt that he'll grow a new one in his R-Phase. He bears his mutilation vaingloriously as a badge of atonement for a sin yet to be committed.

Dick returned to college, graduated, and married a fellow student. They had a son, Carl, in 2014. Ignoring the increasing wealth of details about the evolution of life, Dick preached about Adam and Eve and Noah's Ark. I am a Christian but I know the difference between myth and evidence. Some people would watch elephants parade down the street and deny that a circus had come to town. Blaming myself as a father, I gave Dick up as lost, and of course he thought I was damned. We didn't see each other.

In 2010, when my grandson Jim entered the R-Phase, Roz had had her college degree in biology. During the Food Wars she was a medical student. In 2013, when Bill started to live backwards, she had finished her internship and returned to the study of cytogenetics. But my time was running out. I got her a part-time residency under Dr. Kleiffer while she worked for her Ph.D.

Roz also married a surgeon, Abner McVeigh, in

2015, and they had two daughters, but she continued to work for Kleiffer. He died as if on signal when she took over the Widdick cases.

Now, in 2020, I am sixty again and Roz is thirty-three.

And now, in 2055, you are twenty-five again and she is sixty-eight. I hope she's still alive. She has taken care of you, or me, most of this time. You were very fond of her, and you owe her a lot.

You are on your own again. Good luck.

Note: It's the year 2022, and I am sixty-two and haven't entered the R-Phase. Maybe it happens only once.

Chapter Three

*Robert guessed wrong in thinking that his cycle
would not occur again. He was right about the
need for secrecy. He had been back in the hospital for thirteen years when the family fanatic
brought the R-factor to the government's attention. No one knows what might have happened
if Rosalind and other near descendants had not
conspired against federal law.*

—GABRIEL (D) CHEN, ARCHIVIST

Report on Case
25-W-8309: the R-Factor

14 August 2036
To: Director of Bureau of Genetic Standards
From: Oliver Matusek, Senior Investigator
Subject: Case 25-W-8309, the R-Factor.

Investigation of a claim that certain male members
of a Widdick family possess an "R-factor" on the
Y-chromosome that causes them to enter a state of
amnesia at about the age of sixty and then spend
thirty-five years growing younger until they resume

a new life at the apparent age of twenty-five. The claim was investigated under Section IV, Paragraph 2, of the Munson-Richards Act.

Origin of case:

On 10 December 2035 a man identified as the Reverend Dr. Richard Widdick was referred to the undersigned. He had submitted a Form BGS-C-41, properly executed. He glanced rapidly from side to side as he entered my office and all but threw himself into a chair when I invited him to sit down. He had no left forearm, and I ascertained later that it had been amputated because of wounds he suffered in the Battle of Riverside. I did not ask why he had not attached a prosthetic device, as is normal in such cases. He carried a folder in his right hand, and he tossed it on my desk.

"I've got a big case for the gene police," he announced.

Ignoring his use of a term that the Bureau repudiates, I asked, "Are you referring to the supposed R-factor and its alleged effects, as described in your Form BGS-C-41?"

"Yes!" he exclaimed. "You've got to do something! If you don't, it will spread until the whole human race is damned."

My eyebrows must have risen as I asked, "Damned in what way?"

"It's a sin against God to live longer than a normal lifetime."

"Dr. Widdick," I said, "the Bureau leaves problems of sin to the clergy. We are concerned only with the inheritance of harmful abnormalities. You are a clergyman, are you not?"

"I am, and I have spent many hours on my knees praying that this abomination would be hurled back upon Satan, from whom it came, but God gave man free will to choose the path of righteousness or wallow in wickedness at the cost of his soul." He was talking loudly, preaching at me. "The voice of the Holy Spirit has told me that we must solve this problem ourselves."

I was tempted to give short shrift to someone who heard ghostly voices, but duty compelled me to ask, "What makes you think this R-factor exists?"

"Here," he said. He opened the folder he had thrown on my desk and drew from it a print of an alphamicrophoto. "This is my Y-chromosome. Notice the long extra gene at the tip of the arm above the centromere. That's the R-factor."

I have looked at thousands of chromosomes, and I had never seen anything like it. I was suspicious. "Do you mind if we check your chromosomes at the Bureau?"

"I hope you will. You'll see."

"I'll ask you to go to our lab when we finish talking. Does anyone besides you have this R-factor?"

"There are about twenty of us. I'm not sure exactly. But I am sure that five are in the hospital now growing younger. My father entered the hospital thirteen years ago, and it was his second time. He was one hundred thirty-two years old, so now he's one hundred forty-five."

I almost laughed, but if five men from the same family were in a hospital together with the same problem, a genetic cause was indicated and should be investigated.

"What do you think should be done?" I asked.

"Issue a ruling that the R-factor is prohibited

from inheritance. Sterilize every man who has it."

Voluntary sterilization is common after a man or woman has had two children, but mandatory sterilization is almost never invoked. I looked at him with surprise and asked, "Have you had yourself sterilized?"

"Yes. I had a vasectomy." He buried his head in his hands and muttered, "I confess, to my shame and eternal condemnation, that I had two sons first."

"Well, I will make an investigation."

I obtained from the Reverend Dr. Richard Widdick the names of the men whom he believed were affected, the names of their wives, who should know about such an unusual phenomenon, and information about the hospital and its trustees.

"My sister, Rosalind Widdick McVeigh, is the doctor taking care of the whole nest of vipers," he told me as he was leaving.

Details of Investigation:

1. Preliminary. It was on public record that the Health Research Hospital, in which Widdick males were patients, was operated by the Health Research Foundation, a charitable trust. Trustees were David Widdick, the president of New World Investment Fund, chairman; Dr. Rosalind Widdick McVeigh, a physician and biogeneticist; Leo Widdick, a lawyer; George Widdick, a computer management specialist; and Harry Solway, the president of New World Technology. Both New World Investment Fund and New World Technology are owned by the trust.

The Health Research Hospital is fully approved for both research and the care of patients. It treats amnesiacs and patients who have disorders of known or possible genetic origin. The director of the hospital, Dr. Rutherford Bain, is known for having developed a successful treatment for Alzheimer's disease, which has a genetic source and afflicts its victims with amnesia. His research was sponsored by the foundation.

2. Interview with Mrs. Donna Henlow Widdick, age seventy-five, at her home on 19 December 2035. She is the divorced wife of Robert Widdick and the mother of the Reverend Dr. Richard Widdick. I asked about the latter's claims.

She hesitated, took a deep breath, and exclaimed, "They're true! I'm the one who told Richard about it. I lived for seven years with a man who was a monster." Words poured out of her as if my visit had cracked a dam. "I should have known better. I helped treat Robert Widdick in a hospital for the last two years of his amnesia. I saw him come back to normal, back in 1985, and I married him. But he was ninety-five years old and looked only twenty-five! He was supposed to be sixty-two when he started to lose his memory thirteen years ago, but he was really one hundred thirty-two. Now it will happen again. He'll grow younger and start a third life. It won't matter to me. I'll be dead."

But what sounded like a ridiculous fantasy mattered greatly to her now. "When did you first learn about your husband's condition?" I asked.

"In the hospital. The old one, not the one he's in now. Dr. Kleiffer told me. He was the doctor who took care of Robert. He warned me of what might happen, but I didn't have any sense."

I made a note of Kleiffer's name. "Have you ever told anybody about this?"

"I told my children, nobody else. I couldn't prove it, and I didn't want people to think I was crazy. Besides, I might have broken the law."

"How?"

"Perjury. When we got a marriage license, Robert put down that he was born April 5, 1960, in Rushton, Ohio. I didn't say anything because I thought it was fun to go along with his game. I guess he was the one who perjured himself, wasn't he. But sometimes when I had to fill out something I gave that date."

"Did he have a birth certificate?"

"No. Rushton was pretty much swept down the Ohio River in a flood, and the courthouse was destroyed and the records lost. I never saw his real birth certificate from 1890. He didn't have much from his first life, mainly a few pictures of a wife named Helen, and he took that junk with him when we separated." Suddenly Mrs. Widdick was vehemently bitter. "I wish I could pay him back for what he did to me."

It would have been an odd coincidence for a woman to know one Robert Widdick as a hospital patient and marry a different Robert Widdick. It was more likely to have been the same man, but one born in 1960, not 1890.

"What was supposed to have happened to the original Robert Widdick?" I asked.

"He faked his own death and cremation. Can you imagine that? The papers carried an obituary. Then he pretended to be some kind of cousin of the Widdicks back here. It beats me why they went along with it. He was their ancestor! He had had millions, which were in a trust, and his daughter put the money into the Health Research Foundation. I never saw a penny of it."

Not getting money she had expected would be one reason for bitterness, although she lived in a comfortable house in an upper-income neighborhood. "Is his daughter alive?" I asked.

"She died many years ago. He had a son, Harry, too, by his first wife. Harry went into the hospital in 1985, when Robert came out, and he is supposed to have died fifteen years ago, but I don't believe it."

Nor did I believe in two fake deaths, but it had to be checked.

3. Verification of deaths. The newspapers carried obituaries for Robert and Harry Widdick. Robert, born in 1890, had been founder of the Widdick Tool Co. and had died in 1985 "after a long illness." Harry, born in 1925, had become president of Widdick Tool and had died in 2020, also "after a long illness."

In both cases the remains had been cremated and the ashes deposited in urns in a family plot in a local cemetery. My immediate reaction to that was that it would not be possible to dig up a casket to determine whether it contained a body.

The mortuary that had handled Robert's funeral had gone out of business, and no records remained. The mortuary for Harry was thriving. I interviewed the director, who scoffed at the idea that Harry's death and cremation had been faked.

"We won't handle a person's remains without a death certificate," he told me. "And we don't burn a coffin without checking to be sure the body is in it."

He showed me the death certificate, the record of cremation, and the record of burial of the ashes.

"I'll have to talk to the doctor," I said.

"A doctor would lose his license if he certified a death falsely. Anyway, this one died. They didn't say why, but I happen to know it was cirrhosis of the liver." So he had been an alcoholic. "As for the cremation, I saw the body first myself. I guess it would be possible to bring in a cadaver from a medical school." He laughed at this grisly picture. "Harry's grandson Joseph identified the body. If you want to talk to Joseph, I'm afraid he's in the hospital now, suffering from amnesia."

If these Widdicks were really faking deaths, they were tying up all the loose ends, I thought.

4. Interview with David Widdick, chairman of the Health Research Foundation, on 6 January 2036, at his office for the New World Investment Fund. Mr. Widdick greeted me cordially. "We have an excellent relationship with the Bureau. Our hospital has a contract to do some research for the Bureau, but I suppose you know that." (I didn't.) "What can I do for you?"

I told him I was investigating what I had been told about the R-factor.

"All I know is that we Widdick men do have an extra gene, and we seem to succumb to amnesia at about the age of sixty. We can't find any connection. We don't know what causes the amnesia. If we did, we might be able to prevent it. It's important to me personally because I'll be sixty in five more years. I hate to think of having my life cut short. Years in a hospital don't count."

He was over six feet tall and looked like a former athlete who had not gone to fat, the kind of man who could expect to live much longer than five more years. "But after thirty-five years in the hospital, don't you start over again?" I asked.

He smiled and shook his head. "You've been talking to Donna Widdick or her son, the fire-and-brimstone preacher. I don't know where they came up with that one. My great-grandfather, Robert Widdick, and my grandfather, Harry Widdick, both died after all those years of missing memories."

"Did they grow younger?"

"So it appeared, but it was only an appearance, superficial. They wore out like anyone else."

"Mrs. Robert Widdick claims her husband was rejuvenated and lived a second life starting about the time she married him."

"Ideas like that are one reason he divorced her. The names were the same, but the one she married was only distantly related to my great-grandfather."

"What was their relationship?"

"I don't know. The Robert I know was never in the hospital until thirteen years ago, when he was sixty-two. He came out of Ohio with a reference to the Widdicks here, and they took to him. He was a genius at organization. My uncle, James Widdick, set up the Health Research Foundation, but Robert got the hospital going."

"I notice that four directors of the foundation are Widdicks."

"I should hope so!" he said with a grin. "The foundation was built on Widdick assets. And I will admit a certain amount of self-interest. We picture our role as service to the public, like the gene splicing and implantation of spliced cells that will take over from defective cells and rid the body of certain forms of cancer. But the Widdick men on the board also know that we are likely to spend many years in the hospital, and we want to be sure it's a good one."

"But one director, Harry Solway, is not a Widdick."

"He's the president of New World Technology, which is the main source of money to keep the foundation going. If anybody belongs on the board, he does."

One more thing occurred to me. "Do you have pictures of the two Robert Widdicks?"

He understood, without saying so, that I was making a final effort to discover any evidence that the two Robert Widdicks were the same man. He had his secretary bring in annual reports for the Health Research Foundation for the years 2012 to 2022, the last years in which the second Robert had been president of the foundation, and annual reports for the Widdick Tool Co. for the years 1939 to 1949, when the first Robert had been president of the company and in his fifties. The reports were nearly a hundred years old but had been printed on glossy paper of high quality and remained in good condition.

Comparing photos taken at the same ages, I saw that the two Roberts had looked much alike, with the same high cheekbones, square jaw, and long-lobed ears. The second Robert wore a full beard, and the first was beardless, but a beard is the easiest of disguises. There was one other obvious difference. The first Robert had a half-inch scar on his right temple, as if he had been hit by someone who wore a ring on his left hand. The second Robert had no scar. Well, a scar can be removed easily these days.

"Do you have earlier pictures of the second Robert?" I asked.

David Widdick found one dating back to 1990, when scars could not be easily removed. It showed no scar.

"Thank you," I said without comment, and left.

5. Interview with Dr. Rosalind Widdick McVeigh on 7 January 2036, in her office at the Health Research Hospital. "I understand that you are the doctor for five Widdick men who suffer from amnesia," I said.

"Yes. One of them is my father, Robert Widdick, who entered the hospital in 2022 at the age of sixty-two." She took some records from her desk. "The others are cousins: James Widdick, a patient since 2010; his brother, William, a patient since 2013; and two sons of James, Joseph, who entered in 2033, and Alfred, who became a patient last year."

"Do they grow younger while here?"

"There is no definite answer to that question. James and William look younger than pictures taken of them when they entered the hospital."

"Then why do you say there is no definite answer?"

"Because the first two Widdicks who had this syndrome died. They were an earlier Robert and his son, Harry. Have you grown younger if you die?"

"What is the cause of the syndrome?" I asked.

Dr. McVeigh answered cautiously. "I suspect a genetic factor, but I can't prove it. The Widdicks have an unusual form of amnesia, with a progressive loss of memory, and they also have an extra gene on the Y-chromosome. We can't establish a connection because we don't know what the gene does and we don't know the cause of the amnesia. It could be only a coincidence."

Nevertheless, she had been remiss in her duty.

"As a geneticist, you know the provisions of the Munson-Richards Act and the regulations and directives of the Bureau of Genetic Standards. Why haven't you informed the Bureau of the existence of this extra gene?"

"Because the sample is so small and because the effect of the gene is so uncertain. If you think the gene should be put on record, however, I will send in a report."

"Please do so," I said sternly. Her excuses were not valid. "Include the base-pair sequence of nucleotides in the gene for each of the Widdick patients." The Bureau had already sequenced what the Reverend Dr. Richard Widdick had called the R-factor, which reminded me to ask, "What do you call this gene?"

"The R-factor. That's the name that Dr. Kleiffer, who preceded me here, gave it. R stands for regression."

"Do you have Dr. Kleiffer's records?"

"Yes, and I can dig them up for you. You won't find much about the Widdicks. He was more interested in psychiatric problems that he could alleviate. He knew about the extra gene and told me he suspected a genetic problem, but he doesn't use the term R-factor in his records."

"Please get them for me. Meanwhile I would like to see the Widdicks who are here."

Dr. McVeigh led me through the hospital to a large dayroom in which one male attendant kept an eye on about thirty amnesiacs. The five Widdicks were together. "They know each other," Dr. McVeigh explained, "even though their memories are warped." I asked to talk to James Widdick, who had been there longest, first.

James looked about half the age of eighty-six shown on his admission form. "Do you know why you are in the hospital?" I asked him.

"I don't remember what happened just before I came here, but I remember knowing for years that I might lose my memory someday. That's something, isn't it, remembering that you will lose your memory."

"Do you remember knowing why you would lose your memory?"

His forehead wrinkled as he thought about it. "I remember something about the chance that a loss of memory would be inherited, because it happened to my father and grandfather."

"What is the last thing you remember?"

"A war starting. California and Texas were both invaded from Mexico. Did we win the war?"

"Yes. Thank you, Mr. Widdick."

Interviews with three of the other Widdicks were as brief and uninformative. Finally I talked to Robert Widdick. He was supposed to be seventy-five but looked about fifty, with no gray in his beard. He had no scar and no sign that a scar had ever been removed.

"Can you tell me when and where you were born?" I asked him.

"Let's see." He appeared to be sorting through memories. "It was April 5th, 1960, in Rushton, Ohio."

"Are you sure you weren't born in 1890?"

The question appeared to confuse him. He frowned and hesitated. Finally he said, "How could that be? I was born in 1960. It's 2009 now, so I'm forty-nine."

"The year is 2036, Mr. Widdick," I answered. His

jaw set in stubborn refusal to believe me. "Your wife, Mrs. Donna Widdick, and your son, Richard, say you have lived two lives."

"She's not my wife. I divorced her. Richard is in a Bible college. I didn't want him to go there. I worry about him. Pay no attention to them."

Evidently he still thought he was in the year 2009, to which his memory had regressed. What he said was consistent with a life begun in 1960 and gave no indication of an earlier life. And yet, as I looked at a man of seventy-five who appeared to be about my age, I wondered why these Widdicks would grow younger to no avail, and die. Who ever died of amnesia?

I returned to Dr. McVeigh's office and skimmed the records of the late Dr. Milton Kleiffer, who had treated the first Robert Widdick. His comments about Robert and his son Harry were limited to remarks like "further regression of memory." He wrote nothing about an R-factor.

6. Interviews with four wives of Widdick men who are in the hospital. The wives are Mildred Widdick, age eighty-three, wife of James; Micaela Widdick, eighty, wife of William; Carlotta Widdick, sixty-one, wife of Joseph; and Henrietta Widdick, fifty-five, wife of Alfred. They all said that their husbands had told them that amnesia appeared to run in the Widdick family. Now there seemed to be no doubt about it. Mildred Widdick said she thought she was going to die when her two sons, Joseph and Alfred, followed their father into the hospital. She was worried about three grandsons.

The wives of Joseph and Alfred visited their husbands in the hospital regularly, although they found the confusion of memories frustrating. The older women had stopped visiting their husbands when they could no longer bear to watch the husbands appear to grow younger while they grew older. Yes, they had all heard the story that Robert Widdick was supposed to have lived two lives, but who would believe a silly tale like that? Especially when it came from a vengeful woman like Donna Widdick and her crazy son.

Conclusions:

1. There exists a previously unreported gene on the Y-chromosome of some human males.

2. This gene is probably the cause of an unusual form of amnesia that causes the males to lose their memory regressively while they appear to grow younger at the same rate as their loss of memory.

3. After some thirty-five years of amnesia, the males, who are now about ninety-five years old despite their appearance, die. The report that they begin a new life is not believable, is supported only by testimony from unreliable sources, and is denied by reliable sources.

4. Prior to their period of amnesia, the men live productive lives. They do not become a burden upon society or constitute a danger to it.

Recommendations:

1. That the gene, its position on the Y-chromosome, and its base-pair composition be recorded on the register of the Bureau of Genetic Standards.

2. That the gene be designated Yf for R-factor.

3. That regressive amnesia, with an increasingly youthful appearance, be recorded as the probable effect of the gene.

4. That the voluntary examination of chromosomes of couples who seek licenses to marry, and of unmarried couples who are going to have a child, include determination of whether the men have the Yf gene, and that the prospective parents be advised accordingly under the usual rules of confidentiality.

5. That the routine examination of fetuses include testing for the Yf gene in males, and that the parents be advised of the results.

6. That the R-factor not, repeat not, be considered grounds for obligatory abortion.

7. That Dr. Rosalind Widdick McVeigh be issued a letter of reprimand for not reporting the existence of the gene, but that no additional disciplinary action be taken.

(Note by archivist: Investigator Matusek was methodical and was strict in observing Bureau regulations, but he was too ready to accept self-serving testimony that let him dismiss what he regarded as fantasies. Circumstances were very different when the R-factor drew government attention again. At the time of this early investigation, there was much about the gene that the Widdicks themselves did not know.)

Chapter Four

Some of us forget the feelings of women whose chromosomes lack the R-factor but are the wives or daughters of men who have it. Ironically, for reasons we all know, it is Rosalind who tells us about them. Her report, written during the two years after the federal investigation, also tells of further problems of maintaining secrecy and of keeping the records straight as the family grew.

—GABRIEL (D) CHEN, ARCHIVIST

Comments of
Rosalind Widdick McVeigh (2038)

My reprimand from the Bureau of Genetic Standards rests in the archives of the family with a purple ribbon around it and a gold seal. The board served champagne in my honor when I received it. The Bureau had learned about the R-factor, but only about the amnesia it causes, not the renewed life. I insisted that David share the congratulations, for he had done as much as I to mislead the investigator. All of us had agreed long ago to be frank about the extra gene, if there was an official inquiry, and about the amnesia, for neither could be hidden, but to laugh off any claim of an extra life. Our apparent openness worked.

But we were lucky. I have been rereading the report of the investigator, and we were very, very lucky. The reports are supposed to be confidential, but David got a copy because he knew the director of the Bureau, argued gently that the Widdicks were entitled to know what was said about them, and made a $25,000 contribution to the campaign of the director's candidate for president.

We were lucky because my mother and my dear brother Richard turn people off, and nobody will believe a wild tale coming from the likes of them.

We were lucky that the investigator never guessed that Harry Solway was Harry Widdick living a new life under a new name.

We were lucky that the Widdicks in the hospital, whatever they had forgotten about recent years, remembered that the family secret was meant to be kept secret. I was worried when my father was interviewed because I couldn't guess what memories would be strongest in him, but he remembered that he was supposed to have been born in 1960. I was proud of him.

We were lucky that the two younger wives of men in the hospital were willing to lie, for they knew the full secret. They risked charges of lying to a government investigator, as David and I did.

And we were incredibly lucky that my father had had a visible scar during his first life but none in his second. The investigator seemed half-ready to believe that there was only one Robert Widdick, not two, until he saw the pictures. None of us knew about the scar. Father didn't know himself. No one will ever know how he got it. Apparently he was hit by something that gouged the skin of his temple after he was twenty-five years old, and so he forgot it when he became twenty-five again. The scar must have disappeared when his skin was rejuvenated as he grew younger.

When he starts his third life, he will be Robert Hawkins. He picked the name, although he thought for a time that rejuvenation wouldn't happen to him again. The R-factor didn't take over until he was sixty-two this time, not sixty. Possibly it loses strength. I have read his letter to himself, and I cried when I read about how he loved me and how sad he was that he would forget me and would have to try to recapture his feelings by watching tapes.

James will become James Duval, William will be William Ferrante, Joseph will take the name Joseph Moody, and Alfred will masquerade as Alfred Graham. David, who should be next to enter the R-Phase, in 2041, has picked the surname Mitchell.

We have all been rereading the investigator's report, which was written two years ago, because the Widdicks are under pressure again. Even though I will be doddering around watching men who were old when I knew them emerge young again after their strange hibernation, I am as intent upon their avoiding vulnerability as they are. I like them.

We knew we were in trouble when a zap sheet read by millions came out with a headline:

**REINCARNATION
THE EASY WAY:**
*You don't have to die
to live a second time*

"Two men alive today have lived earlier lives within the past century, and four others are resting in hospital cocoons until they come out as young men again," the story read.

"They are only the first of a growing stream of men who will live again and again, says the Rev. Richard Widdick, well-known evangelist. They include his father, Robert Widdick, and other men in his family.

" 'They have a special gene called the R-factor,' the reverend said. 'It makes them grow back from the age of sixty to the age of twenty-five. They lose their memory while this happens, but then they start out fresh.' "

The story went into detail, including the names of the men in the hospital and my name as their doctor. The sheet hadn't called me for comment but it quoted an unidentified nurse as verifying that the men grew younger. Nurses come and go, and I couldn't guess who she might be.

When the chains and the networks called me to get their own stories, I said that I couldn't discuss my patients, but that Robert and Harry Widdick had died, not lived again, as death certificates would show. I would not allow pictures of the ones in the hospital. When I left work for the day I was startled by the sight of 3-D cameras and reporters waiting for me. At first I wanted to run, but I ratcheted up my courage, touched up my lipstick, patiently let them take all the pictures they wanted, and forced a smile as I gave the same old answers to shouted questions. (The pictures came out well, for a woman of fifty-one, I thought. Not a touch of gray in my brown hair.)

Then I asked for a special meeting of the trustees to determine whether anything else should be done.

"How could the zap sheet write something like that?" George asked. He loves his computers because their electrons race faithfully about their duties with unemotional logic. "Can we sue them?"

"It's not libelous to say someone has lived twice, or will live again," said Leo, our young lawyer. "Half the people in the country think they were kings or queens in a former life. There might be grounds for a right-of-privacy suit."

"I think it would be wiser to let the matter drop," David said. "Let the tumult and the shouting die. If you have to say anything, laugh at Richard's claims. People will forget us when something new and exciting comes along."

David, who was born in 1981, is the oldest active Widdick. In managing investments, he pays close attention to public psychology as well as financial indicators. We have come to rely on his judgment.

Harry is David's grandfather and really the oldest, 113 years old in 2038, but in his new life as Harry Solway, he is forty-three, much younger than his grandson David and little older than his great-grandchildren Leo and George. They are thirty-five and thirty-four. In his second life Harry has had a son, Rupert Solway, who is now twelve, about the same age as Harry's great-great-grandchildren from his first life. Rejuvenation brings paradoxes like that. Since his first life was lived in a different century, Harry looks at things differently from the rest of us.

"Richard didn't tell them we are damned," he said.

"Maybe he did, but they didn't use it," David answered. "The zap sheet keeps its stories short and hits one sensational angle hard. Reincarnation, which is not what happens to us, of course, is exciting. Damnation isn't. Preachers shout about damnation every day."

"I should have known that Richard wouldn't crawl quietly under a rock when the Bureau rejected his complaint," I said. "Probably he didn't know what the Bureau does."

"I wouldn't want to take a test on it myself," George said. They all looked at me.

I kept it short. "The Bureau works to keep harmful genes out of the population. It examines the chromosomes of every fetus at an early stage and puts the chart on permanent record. In certain cases it has the power to order an abortion. If it lacks that power, it may recommend abortion. It also checks chromosomes of people before they are married or looks up their charts and advises them of possible genetic problems in their children. It is defined in law as cruelty to children to let them be born with incurable defects that will make their lives miserable. Opponents of the law say that its real purpose is to prevent such children from becoming burdens on society in these days of overpopulation and slim resources."

"Even if their parents want the children," Leo said softly.

"Yes, but as you know, there are about four thousand genetic diseases. Many of them cause the natural abortion of a fetus long before birth. The Bureau's power to order abortions in other cases is limited. A case of anencephaly is aborted.

The baby would be born missing part of its brain and would soon die anyway. A spina bifida case is aborted because the infant would live in constant pain, undergo drastic surgery, and probably die soon. Cases of muscular dystrophy, sickle-cell anemia, and hemophilia are not aborted because they can be cured. It's left up to the parents whether to abort a female with three X-chromosomes, who will be retarded, or a fetus with Down's syndrome, who has three chromosome twenty-ones instead of two and will also be retarded. The parents usually choose abortion."

"That was an interesting case," Leo said. "The Bureau wanted to abort all fetuses with extra chromosomes on the theory that they did not match the human genotype and therefore were not human. The court ruled, very sensibly in my opinion, that a child of human parents is human."

David grinned and said, "Then I guess a small matter like an extra gene doesn't keep the Widdick men from being human."

We decided to ignore our moment in the hot glare of the public limelight and wait for the light to fade. Over the long run, the birth of children who had the R-factor but not the Widdick name would make the Widdicks seem less abnormal. Three had been born already, Harry's son Rupert Solway in 2026; my bastard nephew, Philip Broadmead, in 2006; and Philip's son Anthony in 2030.

"How about confusing the matter further by adopting boys who will eventually be found to have the Widdick name but not the R-factor?" Leo suggested. "I have a daughter but no sons, and my wife would agree to adopt one."

Having two children these days wins social approval; having more than two is a worse social error than running naked down the aisle at church. Some people have more, especially if they rebel against social norms, but because some children do not survive to have children of their own, and many people have none at all, population is falling. But Leo had forgotten something, and I mentioned it. "The boy will grow old and die, like your daughter, and you will forget him."

They all knew what I was thinking, that I, too, would grow old and die and be forgotten.

"Perhaps I'm selfish," Leo answered. "I'd like both a girl and a boy for the pleasure of watching them grow up in their different ways. They will live normal lives, which can be happy and fruitful. Their children and grandchildren will remember them. So will cousins who grow up with them."

He meant male cousins, of course. The others avoided looking at me.

George changed the subject. Personal matters always made him uncomfortable. "I can't keep track of all the cousins and how everyone is related, and it's going to grow worse," he said, "so I've come up with a system. It's very simple. Everyone with the R-factor has an alphanumeric designator that can be traced by a computer search. Robert, as first in the line, is designated A for his first life and B for his second. Next time out, as Robert Hawkins, he'll be C. Every line starts with Robert. A first son is a 1, a second son a 2. B is added for a second life."

Plainly proud of his simple scheme, he gave us faxes of a list of the male Widdicks, by whatever name they went. Every line carried a name, a designator, the name of the father, the year of birth, and, if a man had entered the R-Phase, the year he did so. The chart brought the males in the family up-to-date as follows:

Robert Widdick, A, 1890–1950

Robert Widdick, B, 1985–2022

Harry Widdick, A-1, son of Robert, 1925–1985

Harry (Widdick) Solway, A-1B, son of Robert, 2020–

James Widdick, A-1-1, first son of Harry, 1950–2010

William Widdick, A-1-2, second son of Harry, 1953–2013

Joseph Widdick, A-1-1-1, first son of James, 1973–2033

Alfred Widdick, A-1-1-2, second son of James, 1975–2035

David Widdick, A-1-2-1, son of William, 1981–

George Widdick, A-1-1-1-1, son of Joseph, 2004–

Leo Widdick, A-1-1-2-1, first son of Alfred, 2003–

Manfred Widdick, A-1-1-2-2, second son of Alfred, 2007–

Peter Widdick, A-1-2-1-1, son of David, 2005–

Rupert Solway, A-1B-1, son of Harry (B), 2026–

Herbert Widdick, A-1-1-1-1-1, first son of George, 2030–

Mark Widdick, A-1-1-1-1-2, second son of George, 2034–

Curtis Widdick, A-1-1-2-2-1, son of Manfred, 2031–

Homer Widdick, A-1-2-1-1-1, first son of Peter, 2032–

Colby Widdick, A-1-2-1-1-2, second son of Peter, 2036–

Richard Widdick, B-1, son of Robert (B), 1989–

Philip Broadmead, B-1-1, first son of Richard, 2006–

Anthony Broadmead, B-1-1-1, son of Philip, 2030–

Carl Widdick, B-1-2, second son of Richard, 2014–

Donald Widdick, B-1-2-1, son of Carl, 2036–

Leo ran down the list, tapping each name with his finger as he counted, and said, "Twenty-two of us now, and the number will grow. We're going to need your computer to keep track of everyone, George."

"It looks to me like there's been an unconscious decision to help sort people out by giving us all different first names," Harry observed. "No matter how many times I need a new last name, my first name will always be Harry. Let's keep new names different as long as we can."

"Good idea," said David. "Just don't ask me to figure out what relation I am to the grandchildren of distant cousins. If the computer knows, that's good enough. Some of your designators are already long, George, with a letter followed by five numbers. What will the list look like after ten generations?"

Naturally my name was not on the list. None of the names of daughters were. "We should put all of Robert's descendants on the computer," I said.

"Have a complete genealogy, men and women. It's all one family. If a man has the R-factor, put a Yf after his name to show that he has the factor on his Y-chromosome. The sons of Robert's women descendants won't have it any more than the women themselves."

In deference to me, the others agreed. I had two daughters and didn't want them left out. George devised a supplementary listing for wives and daughters and the descendants of the latter, showing their connection to a Yf male. Nobody suggested tracing ancestry into the past as most genealogists do. Somebody who wanted a king for an ancestor was welcome to try to find him.

I returned to my work, the ways that I could help patients with genetic disorders and my endless futile search for useful information about the R-factor. We know which gene on the Y-chromosome turns an embryo into a male instead of a female, but we still don't know exactly how it works. How the R-factor gene on the Y works is even more puzzling.

The gene hadn't appeared out of nowhere. Mutations don't produce genes thirty thousand base pairs long, like this one. It had to have come by translocation from another chromosome, where it had been as inactive as many genes are, perhaps after mutation of one or more base pairs in its old location. Like all effective genes, it codes for a protein, in this case an enzyme. The enzyme enters the nucleus of a cell as a trans factor and affects the transcription of genes on the chromosomes. It is similar to the genes that regulate the growth of cells and their differentiation into nerves or muscles or whatever. In this case it increases dramatically the ability to repair all kinds of cells. I could clone the gene but couldn't get it to have any effect on laboratory animals.

Loss of memory was a by-product of rejuvenation. There are a trillion nerve cells in the brain, and billions are involved in memory. As the brain grew younger, the cells would be replaced, which means that they would lose the changes they underwent to store memories. In a second life the cells would form new synapses and accept new memories.

Sometimes when I was depressed over my failure to discover how it all worked, I would brood about the unfairness of women dying while men lived again. Not only myself but my daughters, Julia and Portia, and the wives and daughters of all the Widdick men. The wives and daughters of other men died, I reminded myself. I should not moan about sharing a common fate.

I have talked about this to Carlotta, Joseph's wife, and Henrietta, Alfred's wife. They are sixty-one and fifty-five, and I am now fifty-one. Differences in age mean nothing to friends as one grows older. Both of them had good marriages, and their husbands trusted them and told them the family secret. That doesn't reconcile them to the loss of their husbands and the prospect of living many years alone.

"It's been nearly three years now, and I still haven't gotten used to it," Henny told me recently. "I'm glad to see Al in the hospital, and he's glad to see me, but we're growing apart. He's forgotten that he had a granddaughter two years ago."

"He won't forget you if he comes out again at the age of twenty-five like Robert and Harry, because he was twenty-four when he married you."

"No, and we were madly in love, and it may be good to be remembered like that, but he will have forgotten all of the years we lived together, all that we shared, the house and children, the time our tent was blown away by a hurricane on a camping trip and we clung to each other, drenched, wondering whether we would be blown away, too, or be drowned first. And how proud of him I was when he was president of the state bar."

"Write it all down," I said. "Leave him a cache of pictures and tapes and clippings and other mementos."

Henny shrugged. "Oh, I'll do some of that, but it won't mean anything to him. Robert told me once that it's like hearing the life story of a different person, not oneself. Interesting, but not very, he said. I certainly won't leave him a diary of my old age. I've watched what has happened to Mildred and Micaela. They're too feeble to drive a lectric down the street. They play cards, watch video, and read, but that's getting hard for Mildred, whose eyesight is going. Not having a husband's companionship seems to be the worst part. All they talk about is what happened fifty years ago. Have you noticed that Mildred remembers the happy times, but Micaela thinks about disappointments and fancied insults?"

"Yes. Have you heard that Carlotta is thinking of a divorce so she can remarry for companionship?"

"I've heard. At sixty-one, she'd better hurry. I've been thinking of it myself."

At fifty-five, Henny had better hurry, too, I thought. There weren't many single men the right age whom a woman would want to marry. And Henny had always been plain, made attractive by a lively mind and a pleasant disposition and a winning smile. She didn't smile much anymore.

"Suppose Al comes out in thirty-two years and I'm still tottering around," she said. "Imagine a twenty-five-year-old man married to an eighty-seven-year-old woman! I won't be part of anything so obscene."

"Does it bother you to think of his getting another young wife?"

"Of course it does. Knowing Al, I'm sure he would when he got over the pain of learning that I had died or taken root in a nursing home. We agreed long ago that if one of us died, the other should feel free to remarry, but we weren't thinking of a situation like this. It confuses me."

"It's unfair to the women," I said. "Why should my brother Dick, that all-time champion flonk, live while I die? Why should my Julia and Portia die while Dick's boys live? Your granddaughters are darling girls. Why should they die while your grandson lives?"

"Because that's what people do, dear." She took my hand sympathetically. "Don't blame yourself because your work in the lab can't change things. I was lucky to have grandchildren early, and I expect to have great-grandchildren before I go. I can take pleasure in them and my sons. And don't let me hear anyone call the men freaks."

I suppose I am setting all this down so that it will go in the archives as a reminder to the men, who may come to think that they are superior, not just different, that the women don't like what happens to them, and the big change that fails to happen.

It's unfair.

Chapter Five

During his third lifetime Robert saw weaknesses in the measures taken for family survival. He did not foresee how serious matters would become. He adapted readily to advances in technology. "Gadgets change, but people stay the same," he said, "and people are what count. To Julius Caesar a missile launcher would just be a fancy catapult." In these notes, written midway in his N-Phase, he reviews the situation as he saw it.

—GABRIEL (D) CHEN, ARCHIVIST

Notes by
Robert (C) Hawkins (2075)

I'm pretty sure I won't live forever. I am also sure that I don't want to.

When I tumbled into amnesia for the second time, in the year 2022, I had an effective age of sixty-two. Not bad for a man born in 1890. I lived backwards for thirty-seven years, not thirty-five years like the first time, before I revived again at twenty-five years old in 2059. If I've done it twice, I'll probably do it again, but at what age? Maybe the alternating phases of amnesia and new activity keep stretching out. Maybe the gene that runs our lives grows weaker. If so, old age will eventually catch up with me and I will join the crowd as dust to dust.

So what? How many times must I awaken to despair at learning that Helen, my precious bride, is gone from me forever? We shared a delicious secret when she learned she would have a baby. Did we rejoice when our daughter was born? I've forgotten. How many times must I be a grown man learning the rules of a new world like a kindergarten child? How many times must I look at old pictures of friends, know that I have forgotten them, and wonder how much I am missing by knowing nothing about a life that vanished the way a bubble pops?

Roz has been a consolation.

On that day in 2059 when my mind went back on the common clock, my first memory was that the doctor who had seen me the previous day was named Widdick, too. I had never heard of any Dr. Widdicks, so I went to ask him if I was right.

"Yes," he said. "I'm Peter Widdick. I'm your great-great-grandson."

"And I'm a milk wagon," I answered snappishly. "Don't talk rubbish. My wife is expecting our first child, but I'm a long way from having any grandchildren, and you're nearly twice my age."

"I'm sorry," he said. "I should have eased into this." He pushed a button and said into thin air: "Print summary, Robert." A string of pages skidded out of a slot on his desk. I had never seen anything like it.

"Maybe that little show will convince you it's not the year you remember," he said. "It's the year 2059. You have been here, suffering from amnesia, for thirty-seven years. These papers record it. What's more, this is the second time you've done it. Each time you grow younger and emerge to start a new life."

I didn't know what to answer to a statement so ridiculous, but I thought of events that had puzzled me that morning. First, when I woke up, I found myself in a narrow bed sharing a room with a man I didn't recognize.

"Good morning, Bob," he said.

I frowned as I answered him. "Good morning. Who are you?"

"I'm Joseph. We're in a hospital because we have amnesia. I can remember that because I knew it would happen, but you can't remember it because you didn't know. I won't explain. You would just forget it again."

Mention of a hospital was what had brought Dr. Widdick's name to my mind. Now, in his office, I knew that what he had said about amnesia, at least, was correct.

I followed Joseph past a nursing station into a dining hall. Men and women were having breakfast together. Following Joseph's example, I took a tray made of some lightweight material I didn't recognize, slid it along a rack, and picked fruit and cereal—dry flakes, not the cooked oatmeal I was used to—from a serving counter.

Places had been saved for the two of us at a large table at which there were four other men and one woman. "Hello, Bob," one of the men said to me. I didn't know him either. And then the woman, a good-looking brunette in her thirties, said, "Good morning, Dad."

"Good morning," I answered, not wanting to start the day by calling a crazy woman a liar.

None of them said much during breakfast. A blond man who had only one arm said nothing. They appeared to be confused and trying to get their bearings.

"We remember each other from the years before we were twenty-five," Joseph said. "Sometimes we have trouble matching the faces we remember with what we see as if for the first time each morning. We have little common ground in other memories because they come from so many different early years. We were taught when we were young that this would happen, but we didn't guess what it would be like."

The woman spoke up. "This morning I didn't remember I had seen you yesterday, as I must have done, but I recognized you as soon as you walked in. You look like you did when I was a child."

I wasted no time after breakfast before buttonholing Dr. Widdick. "Who is the woman who called me Dad this morning?" I asked him.

"She is your daughter, Rosalind Widdick McVeigh. You had another daughter who died. You also have two sons, Harry and Dick. They both had breakfast with you. Harry looks sixty years old, and Dick has lost his left arm. They're both in what we call the R-Phase, which you just came out of, and Harry went into it two years ago for the second time. He's the son of your marriage to Helen. Roz and Dick are your children by your second wife, whom you have forgotten."

"What's happened to Helen?" I asked quickly.

"I'm afraid I have to tell you that she died many years ago."

My eyes squeezed shut with anguish at the sudden overwhelming blow. How could Helen be dead? I had seen her yesterday. We had been happy waiting for the birth of our child. How could I face a world so confusing without her?

"I'm lost," I said.

Without Helen, I meant, but he thought I was lost in confusion. That was true, too, of course. "Let me try to explain all this," he said. He gave me a lecture on chromosomes and genes and the R-factor, and on how the R-factor made our lives so different from others. "It's a gene that appears only on the Y-chromosome, so we thought it could be inherited only by men, but by a genetic accident your daughter Roz has it, too."

"Goody for her," I said with indifference.

"You loved Roz very much," the doctor told me sternly. "You have forgotten her, but she still loves you. I hope you will deal with her kindly. She took care of you for years as your doctor here before she slipped into the R-Phase twenty years ago and I came on the job. She's unhappy because you don't know her."

"I'll put on an act. Who were the others at breakfast?"

"I've mentioned your sons, Harry and Dick. Then there are Joseph, your roommate, who is a great-grandson; Alfred, who is Joseph's brother; and David, another great-grandson, who is my father." Dr. Peter Widdick grinned and added, "It should interest you to know that you now have thirty-one descendants who have the R-factor, plus a lot who don't."

"You could say that it interests me," I conceded. I realized that I had begun to believe everything he said. "I'll need a chart."

"I'll order one from the computer. I guess you don't know what a computer is either, but you will, very soon. First I'd like you to read a letter left for you by yourself, as you were ending your second active life, in preparation for this day. I'll see you again this afternoon."

He led me to a small room and left me in privacy. I pick up things fast, but it was hard to grasp everything in the letter in one reading. Two things were important. The Widdicks, mainly me, had set up an organization to take care of our freakish family. Second, I had indeed been very fond of Roz and had suffered pain at the thought of forgetting her. Perhaps, if she came out of the R-Phase too, I could renew our relationship.

I returned the letter to Dr. Peter Widdick and went to a ward room. Among some forty men and women patients the Widdicks formed a cluster of their own, except for Dick, who sat alone lost in his own thoughts. I said nothing, watching them try to establish contact and suffer frustration because their latest memories were of different years.

Roz came up to me and said, "I can't get over how young you look, Dad."

"You look awfully good yourself, Roz," I answered, calling her by name so that she would think I remembered her.

"Thank you. I wish I weren't so confused. I remember starting a medical career, specializing in genetics, but I also realize that I'm a hospital patient, and I don't know why."

"You're in the R-Phase," I said, using the lingo I had picked up from my great-great-grandson, the doctor.

"That's impossible," Roz said. "Women can't inherit the gene that makes it happen."

"Maybe the doctor can explain it." I doubted that he would try, for she would forget what he told her.

But it was the first thing I asked him about when I saw him that afternoon.

"What happened to Roz was similar to a rare genetic accident that produces sex-reversed females," he said. "Remember that chromosomes come in pairs, one from the father and one from the mother. One pair in every cell are sex chromosomes, an X and a Y in a male, an X and an X in a female. When the cells are developing, pairs of chromosomes come together, and the members of most pairs exchange some of their similar genes. That's called crossing over. Sex chromosomes come together, too, but the X and Y in a male are too different for crossing over. All of the chromosomes are duplicated once, and then the cells divide twice. That gives four sex cells, but each sex cell now has only a single chromosome of each kind, not a pair. The four sex cells from a woman will each contain one X. A man will produce two cells with X and two with Y. If a sperm with an X fertilizes an egg with an X, a girl will be born. If a Y fertilizes an X, it will be a boy."

This Dr. Widdick was throwing stuff at me pretty fast, and he waited to give me a chance to ask questions. I felt that I could use a diagram but I had been following him well enough. "Go on," I said.

"Sometimes part of a Y-chromosome will duplicate itself, and the duplicate piece attaches itself to one end. When a man's X and Y move together, the X picks up the tag end of the Y as if it had glue on it. When a sperm with an abnormal X fertilizes an egg, the child will be a daughter with one normal X and one abnormal. She will grow up looking like a woman, but that sliver of Y will keep her from having a woman's internal sexual apparatus.

"Roz is a perfectly normal woman except that she inherited from you an X that had picked up a duplicate of the R-factor gene from a Y. The odds against a duplication on the Y and translocation to an X are enormous, and the chance of having a sperm with an abnormal X fertilize your wife's egg cell is one in a hundred million, but it happened. We code her sex chromosomes XfX, the 'f' meaning R-factor, instead of the usual XX. So now Roz is in the R-Phase. She's growing younger."

Something didn't add up. Roz looked only a few years older than I was now. "The timing is off," I said.

"Very good!" the doctor said with surprise. "She was only fifty-two when she went under, not sixty like a man. I don't know what her effective age will be when she comes out, because she's the first."

I picked up on that. "You mean there are others?"

"Roz has two daughters. One of them, Portia, got a normal X from her. She'll die like most people. The other one, Julia McVeigh Bannister, got an X with the R-factor. They were little girls the last time you went under. Roz never thought to check their chromosomes for an R-factor any more than she saw any point in checking her own. And now

Julia has a daughter, Miranda Bannister, who also has the R-factor."

Thinking of my letter to myself, I said, "So finally it's fair to the women. I don't suppose their sons can inherit it."

"Oh, but they have a fifty-fifty chance. If they get a normal X from their mother, they won't, but if they get an altered X, they will. There's one now, Julia's son, Fred Bannister. He's seventeen. He's an XfY. I'm guessing that the R-factor will work with him, and with any daughters he has, but none of his sons, because he'll pass on to them the normal Y he got from his father."

"I'll have to study up on this," I said. "Definitely I'll need a chart." I thought for a minute. "I have a lot of things to do now that I have a full head of steam again. Where should I start?"

"That's up to the trustees of the foundation. You have a reputation for not being a patient man, but I hope you'll be patient. You have a lot to learn about a world that's very different from the one you remember from 1915. I put in a call after you left this morning, and someone will pick you up in an hour."

My eyebrows rose. "Barely time to say good-bye."

"The others have already forgotten they saw you earlier today. They've forgotten you were in the hospital."

I skipped the good-byes, except to promise Roz, "I'll see you again." She would forget that I had said it, but I wouldn't.

Dr. Widdick took me outside to a strange-looking car, low and rounded, not high and angular. A tall, dark-haired woman sat in the driver's seat behind a window close to the front of the car. The woman got out, and the doctor introduced us. "This is Julia McVeigh Bannister, Roz's daughter. By the way, Robert, remember that your last name will soon be Hawkins." He shook hands. "Good luck."

I miss calling myself Widdick. I know that changing names was my idea, but I don't like it.

Julia and I took our seats, and she showed me how to strap myself in with a seat belt. I did not comment on what seemed to be a nuisance. "Seeing descendants who look older than I am is going to take a lot of getting used to," I said to Julia.

"What do you think it's like for us to see the patriarch of the clan looking still wet behind the ears? You've become a legend, you know."

"That and ten cents will buy me a beer."

She laughed and said, "That and five dollars."

"Oh? What's a living wage these days?"

"Forty dollars an hour would get you by, but just barely."

"Is what I know about machine tools still worth anything?"

"Some, but things aren't made the same way, and we use a lot of glass and ceramics instead of metal. We have to coax most metals out of low-grade ores. Tin and mercury are gone."

"How does a good-looking woman like you know about things like that?" I asked.

Julia pulled the car to the side of the road and stopped. "I'm going to start your orientation with one stiff lesson right now. Drop any antique ideas you have about women who shouldn't worry their pretty little heads about matters that ought to be left to men. For any job that doesn't require bonehead muscle power, women do as much as men and do it as well. I know about metals because I'm a resource manager." She looked at me slyly. "Brace yourself. The president of the United States is a woman."

I threw up my hands as if in horror and said, "Women must have won the vote."

Julia laughed. "You really are out-of-date."

Our car ran almost silently. I could hear the hum of the tires but no engine noise. Julia explained that the car was a "lectric," powered by batteries. That required a further explanation. Oil wells had been pumped dry. Oil derived from oil shales and tar sands was reserved for heavy machinery and military vehicles, like tanks, and certain plastics. Julia apparently assumed that I knew what plastics were. Aircraft, even the rigibles, which I gathered were powered balloons, used jets from the ignition of solid fuels, like rockets under control. There was still coal for fuel, but most power was electric, and most of that was converted from energy from the sun. I would see a lot of people on bicycles and some on horses.

"Spaceships lift off with chemical fuel and switch to nuclear," Julia said.

"Spaceships?" I asked in surprise.

"An international team landed on Mars twenty years ago, and we are gradually assembling a base there. We service it from our base on the moon."

We stopped at a gate in a stone wall that carried a sign reading New World Enterprises. A guard stood there, but I didn't see him do anything while the gate opened, as if the gate itself had checked Julia's identity somehow. "The board of the Health Research Foundation, which you set up to run Widdick affairs, usually meets here," Julia said.

"Five men and me. They called a special meeting to welcome you."

The first thing I saw when I entered the room was a large portrait of what looked like me, but much older, which must have been copied from a photograph. Five men who had been seated in leather-backed chairs around a walnut table rose when I entered.

"This is Leo Widdick, our chairman, who is a lawyer and a great-great-grandson of yours," Julia said. "He was born in 2003, and you knew him as a youth in your second N-Phase." Leo looked at me with intense curiosity and shook my hand.

Julia took me around the table. "George Widdick, who is also your great-great-grandson, is a computer expert. You will need to know a lot about computers, and George will teach you. He was born in 2004. Manfred Widdick is Leo's younger brother, born in 2007. He runs New World Enterprises."

Three men in their fifties. They would be looking at me as an example of what would happen to them after a dreary time in the R-Phase that would begin in a few years.

They already had two examples in front of them, I discovered. "And here are two grandsons, old friends whom you've forgotten," Julia said. "Remember your letter to yourself? We've all read a copy in the family archives. These are James and William, who worked with you to set up the foundation."

They looked more like me than the others, although all of them had high cheekbones and strong jaws. They smiled when they shook hands. "Just as you are Robert Hawkins now, James has become James Duval, and William is William Ferrante,"

Julia said. "We have succeeded in keeping the restoration effect of the R-factor from becoming publicly known. James is a lawyer again, and William runs the clone works."

"Whatever that is," I commented.

"It's where we duplicate genes for medical purposes, like churning out hormones, or to develop better plants and animals," William said. "We also work with old stuff that's simpler. Take a cow that gives a lot of milk. She is inseminated by a prize bull. We take one of her fertilized eggs when it develops to the sixteen-cell stage and remove the nuclei from the cells. We trade these for nuclei in the eggs of sixteen ordinary cows and implant each egg in a uterus. They grow and are born as sixteen identical calves."

"That's all abracadabra to me," I said. "Take me over the bumps again when I've learned the basics. One thing. Can you do it with people?"

"We could, but it's against the law, which is enforced by the gene police."

I shook my head at another meaningless term and turned to James. "Did you just pop out of the hospital and start practicing law again?"

"Hardly," he said with a laugh. I remembered reading that I had liked him. "I had finished law school by the time I was twenty-five the first time around, but as James Duval I needed a new degree and knowledge of changes in the law. I worked for Leo here for a while, and with the help of some fake credentials, I got into law school for the second time."

"With forged diplomas?" I asked.

"You could call it that. All schools and colleges keep their records in computer memory. George here can invade almost any computer and change its memory to concoct an imaginary transcript on demand. His son Herbert can do the same trick."

Herbert will take over when George enters the R-Phase, I thought. Fakery had to be planned, and ssed as rarely as possible and as delicately as possible, to keep the family secret. It took organization. My descendants appeared to be a capable lot. Where would I fit in?

"Do you have plans for me?" I asked.

"You'll stay with me for a couple of weeks," Leo said. "My wife is dead, my daughter is married, and so is an adopted son. Maybe next time I'll have a son of my own. After two weeks with me the old Robert Widdick who came out of the hospital will die, officially, and the new Robert Hawkins will move into a condo in the same building that Julia and her family live in."

What was a condo? I would find out soon. I had taken a shine to Julia and was glad I would be near her.

"We'll all see a lot of you," Leo continued. "We'll show you around and teach you how things work these days so you can go out on your own among strangers and not seem quarky. Then Manfred will find a fast-track job for you in New World Enterprises."

Unless I found something I'd rather do. They would learn I was hard to push. But I was glad that they would ease the way before I staged my comeback.

While I was learning about computers and lasers and glass wires and sun-power satellites and space flight and about new countries from Armenia to Zend and about the nuts and bolts of existing in an unfamiliar world, like how to call up a catalog on my screen and order just about anything to be delivered by robot from a warehouse, I spent many evenings with Julia. She drilled me on Spanish words that had come into American language. "Friends" were "amigos" and "firemen" were "bomberos." She also reminded me of something I hadn't noticed.

"How are your teeth?" she asked one night.

"Fine. Why?"

"Remember your letter to yourself? You said you had false teeth. While you were in the R-Phase, a technique was developed for implanting buds that would grow into new teeth. You got a full set."

I ran a finger over my teeth. They were all there, including wisdom teeth. "I guess you don't notice things unless something's wrong," I said.

"You just about have to cut off a head these days for something you can't replace. We keep offering to graft a new arm on your son Dick, but he keeps refusing. I think we're in for trouble when he gets out again."

We talked a lot about the R-factor and how it affected the people who had it. "How do you feel about having it yourself?" I asked Julia.

"Mixed. Roz, my mother, had to go to the hospital when she was only fifty-two. She was entering menopause, and that may have triggered it. But fifty-two! That's hardly long enough to see your children grow up. And we don't know how old she'll be when she comes out. Suppose she's twenty-two, and suppose I follow the same pattern. A good fresh start, but I don't like to think of spending thirty years forgetting things first."

"The worst part is knowing how much you've forgotten when you make the fresh start," I answered. "Maybe it's better than forgetting everything permanently in a graveyard."

"I'm glad my sister Portia doesn't know I have the R. She doesn't have it. She's already bitterly jealous because I was married and she wasn't."

Squabbles were natural in a family as large as mine had become, but those who had the R would stick together, I thought. At least they ought to. Dick's sons and grandsons had the R but had little to do with the rest of us. They knew that the family didn't like Dick. Nevertheless they were my descendants, and I wanted to meet them and strengthen family ties.

Soon after some derelict's ashes were deposited in a grave with my name on the marker and I had enjoyed a memorial service at which Leo recited my eulogy with a straight face, the trustees indulged me by setting up trips for me to meet Dick's descendants. Julia went with me. We enjoyed a leisurely trip in a rigible, in cabins more comfortable than Pullman berths, to San Diego, where Philip Broadmead, the bastard son whom Dick had rejected, was an aircraft mechanic. I was glad that screwdrivers and wrenches were still used in this electronics age.

"I want to caution you about one thing," Julia said before we met Philip. "Please don't tell him your last name is now Hawkins. Last names for new N-Phases are revealed only on a need-to-know basis. It's a security measure adopted by the trustees."

I didn't like that, but I saw the point. Suppose somebody got drunk and blabbed, or had a row with his wife and she blabbed. They might have heard about revivals but couldn't prove anything without knowing the names.

Julia introduced me to Philip as "your grandfather, Robert Widdick."

"You're just a kid," Philip objected. He was fifty-three now.

"As you will be again someday," I answered. "I wanted to see how you are getting along."

"Just fine, no thanks to the Widdicks," he said as if holding a grudge. "I was grown-up and working before I was let in on the family secret, and it was too late to get on the track for big bucks like the cousins my age. It was a tight squeeze putting my son, Tony, through college, but I did it, and on my own."

I had gone into the R-Phase when Philip was sixteen years old, but the foundation should have seen to it that he was subsidized. That was one improvement in family arrangements that I would see was made. "I never went to college," I said. "Do you want to try a different career next time around?"

"Not if they still need mechanics. I like working with my hands."

He sounded defiant, as if hiding resentment. But as we talked it became clear that he was proud of his son, Anthony Broadmead, who was an engineer in the space program.

Tony was next on my list. He was quiet and serious, twenty-nine years old, only four years older than I had become again.

"I want to go to Mars," he said. "I design life-support systems for an environment that makes

Death Valley look like Eden, but I want to help put them together and see how they work."

"I'm betting you'll make it," I said. "Good luck." This was a man of my own stripe. He had his grandfather Dick's single-minded dedication but had given it a productive channel.

After his two daughters had gone to bed and his wife had wandered into another room, we talked about the R-factor. "I want to come back to make sure my daughters and their families are making out all right," he said. "After all, they have only one chance at life."

Julia shifted in her chair and warned me with a glance not to mention that she and her mother and daughter had the R. Next day I asked her if parents couldn't choose to have a son if they wanted one.

"Couples can choose the sex of their children every time, if they want to, because techniques have been developed to segregate sperms containing Y-chromosomes from those with X," Julia said. "But many people find going to a lab distasteful. They'd rather take a chance. You might think that Widdick men would want to concentrate on sons, who would carry their extra gene, but they know they're missing the pleasure of having a little girl if they don't have one."

"Don't they know they'll forget her next time around?"

"I don't think that sinks in until it happens."

Julia flew home to take care of neglected work while I went to a farm in Canada to see Dick's legitimate son, Carl, and Carl's son, Donald. Carl had been eight years old when I went into the R-Phase in 2022. As a teenager he had run away from home and a father who talked about nothing but a family curse. Now, at forty-five, he grew wheat with the help of Donald, who was twenty-three. Descendants who were older than I seemed to be still upset my balance; I liked them younger.

Carl and Donald were bigger than I am, and muscular. Machinery that they had to explain to me filled a large adobe brick shed with a plastic roof. Robot-controlled drills could plant wheat in perfectly straight lines, eight rows at a time. Combines used radio signals and close-range sensors to harvest the same rows. All this didn't save a farmer from plain hard work. Both were married, Donald only this year. He and his bride lived in a separate house on the farm. Carl and Donald introduced me to their wives as a cousin.

They gave me a tour of the farm, on horseback to save fuel, to show me what they were accomplishing, and so that we could talk in private. So far as I knew, I had never been on a horse before. I enjoyed it except for the jarring my spine took as I bounced up and down when the horse trotted.

"The Widdicks are a large family, and we're getting out of touch with each other," I said. "That's one reason I wanted to meet you. Do you ever regret living so far from the others?"

"What would we talk about?" Carl asked in turn. "They don't know farming. I don't know law or medicine or manufacturing. All I know about computers is how to use my own to handle my bank account and order supplies and keep track of the price of wheat and sell it at the right time. We have friends here."

"Why Canada?" I asked. "Why not Kansas?"

"You been to Kansas?" Donald asked. "Changes in the weather have made Kansas too hot and dry to grow wheat."

After supper Carl's wife apologized for not having a robot to clean off the table. She and Donald's wife went to the kitchen to feed dishes into a machine to scrape and wash and dry them.

"So you're my great-granddaddy," Donald said. "How long have you been around?"

"Since 1890, off and on," I answered as dryly as if I had been quoting the price of wheat.

"It's hard to believe. I feel I should take you out and introduce you to a couple of good-looking young women."

The vision of Helen that rose in my mind made me catch my breath. "Thanks, but I'd rather not." In time they, too, would remember only the first years of their marriages. "How much do your wives know about the Widdicks?"

"They know that we inherit a strong likelihood of amnesia at about the age of sixty," Carl answered. "They know that a family foundation will then pay for our care. We signed marriage contracts that call for divorces when the foundation takes over. My share of community property will go into a trust for Don, with my wife to receive the income during her lifetime. Don's wife will have the same setup. All of the Widdicks sign similar marriage contracts now."

The trustees hadn't told me that. They probably hadn't filled me in on a lot of things yet. The marriage contracts calling for divorces when amnesia set in were a good idea. The wives would be free to marry again, if they wished. When the husbands started new lives, they could marry again without being bigamous. It might be better for them not even to see wives who had aged thirty-five years while they were growing younger. Too painful for both of them.

Next I visited the other Widdicks who had an assumed name derived from my son Harry, who had become Harry Solway his second time around. His son Rupert had become a doctor and would take over the Widdick cases when Dr. Peter Widdick, who had ushered me out of the R-Phase, went into it himself. We needed a reliable supply of doctors.

With the Broadmeads, Solways, James (B) Duval's family, William (B) Ferrante's family, and my own new name of Hawkins, there were now five names besides Widdick for children born with our fancy gene. William had a son, Jeff Ferrante, now four years old. Rupert had a son, Michael Solway, who was two.

I assumed that I would eventually marry again, if only to spread the R-factor, and start a Hawkins line. Other new names would surface from their hospital stays soon.

I almost forgot two. Julia's seventeen-year-old son, Fred Bannister, had the R on his X-chromosome. Her daughter, Miranda, had it on one of her Xs and might have children by a husband with a different name. She was nineteen now.

Other Widdicks remained Widdicks. Manfred's son Curtis was in training as a space pilot. He had a son, Ezra, who was three. Peter had two sons, Homer, who was another doctor, and Colby, who was an army infantry officer. Homer had a five-year-old son, Eugene. He was my first great-great-great-great grandson, and I had lived to know him! He was skinny but strong, and he had begun to read. Besides Herbert, who had followed his father into computers, George had had a son Mark who had died at the age of four when he climbed over a fence and drowned in a swimming pool. And now Herbert had a two-year-old son, Charles.

Keeping track of all my descendants was as confusing as watching marbles spill out of a pouch. I don't know why I felt responsible for them. If I had died a normal death, I wouldn't be. But I had entered a third lifetime and was surrounded by men and women and children who carried my abnormal gene. I could see problems developing. The trustees met to hear my concerns.

"I have had a chance to look around, and I think you have all done a remarkably good job," I told them. They beamed as if they forgot that I was as young as I looked and they saw a patriarch wise in his judgments. "I have also tried to look into the future. The family is growing apart, and I think the time will come when we need tightly linked support. How can we encourage closer bonds? Second, the number we need to care for in the hospital is growing. There are six today; in ten years two will come out and six will go in, so there will be ten. Should we consider a new arrangement?"

That caught their attention, for all six of the trustees knew that they would be the ones to enter the hospital, one by one, starting with Leo four years from now.

"The most important problem is what we will do when our secret becomes publicly known. That's bound to happen someday. We don't know what the public reaction will be. We can be certain that the gene police won't like it."

"We need someone on the inside there," Leo said reflectively. "Someone in administration who can tell us what's held in the local net and possibly influence policy."

"Take it a couple of steps further," James said with a grin. "I like the idea of having the Widdicks take over the Bureau of Genetic Standards."

Leo laughed but said, "They check the chromosome map of job applicants. They would never take someone with the R-factor on his Y-chromosome."

Julia had the answer. "My daughter Miranda doesn't have a Y. My son Fred does, but his R is on his X and hasn't been found because nobody was looking for it there."

We favored Miranda because she was two years older than Fred and could infiltrate the gene police two years sooner. At nineteen she wanted a career in biogenetics and had begun her studies. She didn't yet know about the R-factor.

"I'll tell her immediately," Julia said. "She'll be fascinated. And she has a romantic streak that will make the idea of being a secret agent appeal to her."

Fred's turn to help would come when he fathered children named Bannister, not Widdick, who had the R.

To keep the family together, I proposed that we buy all of the land around a lake somewhere for a private summer resort for free vacations. "Let the children and teenagers have fun together while they're young and they'll never forget each other."

"For all of the family, non-Rs as well as Rs," Leo said, and I remembered that Leo's son was adopted. Non-R cousins, too, I thought, for they shared descent from me, and someday we might need their goodwill. I hadn't yet looked up the family of my daughter Jane, who had been so helpful to me during my first revival. Probably I should not introduce myself but simply find out discreetly if they needed anything.

For a better place to care for Widdicks in the R-Phase, who would soon be too numerous to be hidden among other patients in a hospital, I suggested a private clinic where they would receive the minimal care they needed. It should be isolated but near a community that could provide workers.

"I would phase it in, because people would wonder why, if all the Widdicks were moved at once. Start with Joseph and Alfred, James's sons. They get along well. Then the others, a year or two apart. Except Richard. We should try to keep the location a secret, and I don't trust Dick."

"You run scared," James commented.

"Look at the record."

My other concern was a certain unwieldiness that had developed in the management of the trust and New World Enterprises. We had added not only the clone works, in the biogenetics department, but a factory to make spacecraft components, a computer factory, under George, and even a factory for household appliances in China. New World Enterprises was the largest privately held company in America. Manfred was in charge, overall, and the others knew what was happening only when he told them.

"I've figured out some things I could do," I said. "Let me set up a summer place in Wisconsin or Minnesota and get a clinic started, maybe in the Adirondacks. Then I suggest that you make me staff director for this board of trustees. Manfred and I could set up a system for reports on a regular basis, and I would keep you all informed. I would also take charge of our archives, keep them up-to-date, and work with George on better security."

The others looked a little surprised that a man who had established a machine-tool business by the age of twenty-five would want what sounded like a clerical job. Manfred resisted funneling reports through me. I saw that he was afraid of losing control, but I argued that he would have more time for the important problems of running our enterprises if I made the necessary extracts from the data his managers gave him. He joined the others in agreeing to my proposals. I knew that I would be at the center of affairs and eventually be running them.

For about fifteen years, everything went smoothly. Births continued to add to the family. Everyone enjoyed swimming, sailing, fishing, and games at the summer compound set up around Lake Miniwoc. There were no deaths among the Rs, only long years of incapacity during rejuvenation. By 2069, when Julia followed the other trustees who had greeted me into the R-Phase at the isolated treatment center I had established, I was chairman again, younger than the others. Two things more important to me had happened.

It took seven years for memories of Helen and my feeling of loss to fade. The time came when I could watch a robot wheel itself over a carpet and suck up dirt freed by sonic vibrations without thinking of Helen beating a rug hung on a clothesline. Meanwhile I had grown fond of Becky, whom I had met at a political fund-raiser. Perhaps she sensed my loneliness; perhaps she responded to my insistence on thorough political organization down to the ward and precinct level. Let others take care of a candidate's image. She didn't realize that I was putting politicians in my debt.

Becky moved in with me, a custom that I still found hard to accept despite its advantages. She became Mrs. Robert Hawkins, without knowing the truth about my background, in 2066. A year later our son Vernon was born. That's when I told Becky about the R-factor. She forgave me for delaying the omission. Maybe she thought I was joking.

"You always seemed normal to me," she said. "Above average, but normal."

Roz came out of the hospital in 2069, apparently twenty-two years old again. Her new name was Rosalind Harper, and she was supposedly from Vermont, come to the city to enter medical school with a beautifully faked college transcript. I soon learned why I had been fond of the Roz I had forgotten. She remembered enough genetics to understand immediately how she had inherited the R-factor, and she plunged into contemporary biogenetics with the glee of a fish returned from a fishbowl to a river. And she still loved me as a father.

Roz had only two months with her fifty-two-year-old daughter, Julia, before Julia took her turn in the renewal center. She called on her there to cheer her up and learn about the years of Julia's life that she had missed. Roz avoided her other daughter, Portia, age fifty, unmarried and sour, for she had no excuse to see her without revealing our secret beyond a secret, the fact that a woman could inherit the R. Roz was able to delight in her grandchildren, Miranda and Fred Bannister, and in their children. Her pleasure in the latter was alloyed with sadness and resignation that two of the great-grandchildren would die.

Miranda, who was using high-tech lab equipment to map genes for the Bureau of Genetic Standards by now, had married a man named Moley. Their daughter, Angela Moley, had inherited Miranda's R. But their son, Kyle, had inherited his mother's normal X-chromosome and a normal Y from his father. Fred Bannister's first child, a girl, was born in 2069, the year Roz came back to normal. Roz herself checked the baby's chromosomes and found that she had the R. This was the first evidence that a man with an Xf would pass it on to his daughters. Fred's son, Jerry, born in 2071, got his father's normal Y and one of his mother's normal Xs. No repeated lives for him.

The rest of us were reminded of our mortality by a family tragedy. Curtis Widdick, my great-great-great-grandson, was killed on a flight to Mars in 2072. I was among those who proudly watched the launching and heard him say that a spaceship was "safer than skates." Large meteoritic rocks with orbits that crossed space between Earth and Mars were charted, but not small ones. The accident that everyone thought had little chance of happening, happened to Curt. A rock that weighed only about two thousand kilograms smashed through the hull of his ship, and his body exploded as air burst into space.

His wife and his two sons, Ezra, age sixteen, and Enoch, twelve, had also cheered the launch.

In 2075 there are forty-one Widdicks who go by various names, not counting the two who died. I wait warily for the year 2084, when my trouble-some son Richard will come out of the hospital.

A father never loses hope for a son, and I have persuaded the other trustees to try to rehabilitate him, to make him feel a part of the family. If we have misjudged him, we will pay for it.

Chapter Six

Richard Widdick can be tagged with an old phrase that is still current: "An accident waiting to happen." Or a time bomb waiting to go off, because of what he did to the family. We can understand his twisted mind, which has found a place in textbooks on psychology, and we are bemused at thinking about how much talent was wasted. Like his father, he was single-minded and kept his own counsel, and he was a born leader, but how different were their goals! He was unlike Robert in that he was vain and wanted fame. Let him speak for himself.

—GABRIEL (D) CHEN, ARCHIVIST

Testament of
Richard Widdick (2086)

I was too clever for them.

I found myself in a large room with nine strangers who avoided me. It seemed to me that I had just returned from preaching a sermon on the tortures of Hell that had wrung sobs from my congregation and public repentance from ten sinners.

Suddenly I was here! What was this place? Who were these people? They all seemed to know me. One of them was a woman, who moved away without a word when I came near.

I did not tell the others of my bewilderment. I listened to them talk about things that meant nothing to me. Sometimes they called each other by their first names, which were not enough for me to identify them.

Once one of them said to another one, "I wonder what Robert's up to these days."

The other one glanced at me and answered, "Probably waiting for him to come out."

Who was Robert? Could they mean my father?

A nurse wearing white arrived and escorted me to a doctor's office. "How are you today, Richard?" he asked.

"All right. Who are you?"

"I am Dr. Rupert Solway. Tell me what year this is."

"It's 2014."

He sighed and asked, "What else do you remember?"

"My church work. And my wife, Luanna, and the baby she had last month, Carl." I raised the stump of my left arm and said, "I remember this, too."

After consulting notes on his desk, he looked up at me and said, "You won't be seeing me much longer."

"What does that mean?"

"You'll probably forget it, but I'll tell you. It's the year 2084. You've been here thirty-five years and will leave very soon. Do you remember the R-factor?"

Instantly I understood what had happened. Ripples of horror lapped at me like a tide washing across driftwood. I had fallen victim to the Widdick curse. No matter how vigorous I felt and what I remembered, I was not twenty-five years old but ninety-five and doomed to live on far past the divinely allotted span of man's years, doomed and damned.

By the grace of the Holy Spirit I suppressed my feelings and said only, warily, "I remember it." I had known about the R-factor since boyhood.

"This is the clinic where the family takes care of members when they succumb to amnesia and grow younger," Dr. Solway said. He looked at his notes again. "It's about time for you to start remembering things from day to day. If you remember this conversation tomorrow, we'll talk about your future. You can go back to the others now."

I said nothing, but I would not leave this place until I had learned as much as I could. Surely the Lord had not condemned me to this fate because I had lapsed in faith. Surely I had tried to warn the world against the Widdicks and our demonic gene. If so, I must have failed. This could be a second chance.

It was a family clinic, Dr. Solway had said, so the others in it must be Widdicks. I had to find out who they were. I went up to the youngest man, who seemed to be in his thirties, and said, "I seem to have forgotten who you are. What's your name?"

"Harry Solway." He grinned maliciously, as if he knew something I didn't.

I had never heard of him. What was a Solway doing in a clinic for Widdicks? I remembered the name of the doctor who had just seen me and asked, "Are you related to Dr. Solway?"

"I never heard of a Dr. Solway."

He could have forgotten, I thought. "What year is this?" I asked.

"It doesn't matter what year I think it is, does it?"

That was enough to show that he understood the regression of memory that afflicts the Widdicks. What somebody named Solway was doing here remained a puzzle. "I suppose not," I said, and looked around.

It occurred to me that the oldest man present, a man in his late fifties, looked like a cousin I had seen occasionally during my youth, before I turned away from my family with loathing. I went to him and asked, "Are you James Widdick?"

He hesitated before answering, "No. I am James Duval."

Another non-Widdick name, which puzzled me further. I pursued my questions with others and felt grimly rewarded by men who gave their last names as Widdick. They were Leo, George, Peter, and Manfred. My memories of 2014 and earlier years included the memory of hearing about them as boys. I was grim because my prediction that the family curse would spread was confirmed. Only Peter showed some sympathy for me in my confusion.

"Don't worry about names," he told me. "It will all be clear to you soon."

I decided to confront two men between forty and fifty years old who had stayed across the room from me. Approaching them, I said, "You two act as if you had a grudge against me. Who are you?"

The younger one exploded in a short, harsh laugh, and said, "Surely you remember your own sons."

I gaped at them. Such an unexpected and oppressive reminder of my sinfulness couldn't be possible, but of course it was. The older one must be Philip, whom I had abandoned for eventual adoption by a man named Broadmead. No, he would appear to be the younger one, for he had been born first and would have succumbed to the R-factor first. He would have been eight years old in this year of 2014 in the regression of my memory. And Carl, my legitimate son, had just been born.

"Philip," I said hesitantly. I had been careful to have nothing to do with him, but my father had told me about that girl who had tempted me, and her marriage to Broadmead.

"Yes," he answered. "Philip Broadmead, not Philip Widdick. I owe you nothing, not even courtesy. I don't remember my yesterdays here, but for all I know we have repeated this scene every day for the eighteen years I must have been here. By my calculation, you entered the R-Phase in 2049 and should soon be out of it. I'll be glad to be rid of you."

He turned his back on me. I didn't recognize the term R-Phase, but I understood it. If he resented seeing me, I detested the sight of him, living proof of my inherited guilt. The same for Carl, if the other man was indeed Carl.

"And you are Carl," I said to him. He nodded, and I continued, "I remember you only as a very small baby."

"But I remember you as a fanatic," he said coldly. "You were full of crazy ideas, and you were a father who beat me for what you called the good of my soul. 'Spare the rod and spoil the child,' you would say. Do you remember that I ran away from home at the age of sixteen? No, of course you don't."

I would have walked away, but I had to ask one question. "Do you have children? Grandchildren?"

Guessing what concerned me, he said, "Never fear, father, the R-factor is spreading."

Interviewing Philip and Carl had filled me with revulsion and despair. I felt like brooding alone, but I still had to find out what a woman was doing here. She was tall and a bit stout, and I had seen her watching me as I talked to the others. She smiled a small strange smile when I asked her name.

"Julia McVeigh Bannister," she answered.

None of the three names meant anything to me. I went straight to the point: "Why are you here?"

"You don't know me, Richard Widdick, but I know all about you, and I will tell you nothing."

Plainly I had aroused much hostility in those years that I had forgotten. I began to think of what I must do to be more effective in my crusade. I must dissemble, hide my convictions, until I had enough information to act.

In the afternoon I returned to Peter Widdick, the man who had shown tolerance, if not friendliness. "My memory is back," I said. "I remember all of my conversations this morning clearly. All of us here have the R-factor, don't we?"

"That's why we're here."

So the woman, Julia McVeigh Bannister, had it, too. I didn't understand how a woman could inherit a gene from a man's Y-chromosome, but I had a more pressing question. "I know that my father

was in"—and I used my newly acquired phrase—
"the R-Phase before I was born. Did he go through
it again?"

"Indeed he did. I was his doctor for a while."

"What is he doing now?"

"How could I know that? My memory has gone
back to the year 2046, which is before he would
have come out."

"Sorry," I apologized. "I'm still not used to the
way our senses of time don't mesh. Perhaps you
could tell me why people named Solway and Duval
and Bannister are in with the Widdicks."

"It will be up to someone else to tell you that."

I had learned that a man could be rejuvenated
more than once. No doubt he would transmit his
damnable trait again each time. It appeared unlikely
that I could learn anything more from my fellow
patients. It was time to leave.

Next morning when I saw Dr. Solway I told
him that I had recovered my memory and repeated
word for word our conversation of the day before.
I named my fellow patients and added that I knew
that two of them were my sons.

"Very good," he said. "You're ready to leave.
I'll make arrangements to have you picked up and
begin your orientation to a society that is very different from what you remember."

Most questions could wait, but I asked one. "What
relation are you to Harry Solway?"

"He's my father."

If Harry had the R-factor, so did his son, Rupert.
How widely had the R-factor spread, and had the
gene appeared in people who weren't Widdicks?

In the afternoon I was taken to a courtyard inside
walls around the clinic. A small helicopter like

a dragonfly waited. Two propellers revolved lazi-
ly, idling, in the wings and another in the tail.
Standing beside steps to the cabin was a woman whom I recognized instantly, with surprise, as
my sister.

"Rosalind!" I exclaimed.

"Right," she said. "Hop in, Richard."

After I took a seat in the cabin she sat beside
me behind a wheel, from which the upper third of
the rim had been removed, and a control board. We
looked each other over. If I was ninety-five, Roz
was ninety-seven, but she appeared to be in her
thirties compared to my present apparent age of
twenty-five. Somehow the difference in ages had
increased.

"You're looking good, Roz," I said, beginning
my campaign.

"Thank you. So are you." She reached past the
wheel and pushed a button. The aircraft rose several
thousand feet and turned without her touching the
wheel.

"I didn't know you could fly a plane," I said.

"Anybody can handle a flier. Just tell the computer where you want to go."

I looked down at lakes and forested mountains,
like what one would see from over upstate New
York. "Where are we going?" I asked.

"To Cornell, where I do genetic research. I live
outside Utica, where it's quiet and I can ease you
into the modern world."

"Who arranged for all this?"

"The trustees of the Health Research Foundation.
Do you remember the foundation?"

"That was Dad's project." Casually I asked, "Is
he still active in it?"

"Very much so." Roz stared at me without expression and asked, "How do you feel about the R-factor now that you're starting out again?"

She wouldn't believe me if I pretended to have lost the feelings that had been so strong in me, so I answered cautiously. "I have to do a lot of thinking about that."

"That's a start. Here's another one. Your name is now Richard Hardy."

"You don't say." It burst out of me as I bristled at assuming a fraudulent identity. "What's yours?"

"Rosalind Harper Touhy."

"Where did you get a name like that?"

"Harper was picked for me when I surprised everyone by going into the R-Phase. We all take new names when we come out. Touhy is my married name. My husband teaches history. We have a boy who's twelve and a girl who's nine. Don't tell them about the R-factor. They're too young. You are supposed to be a cousin, a graduate student who is writing a dissertation in history."

All the history that anyone needed to know was in the Bible, I thought, but I'll play their game. At the moment two things seemed important. If everyone who came out of the R-Phase took a new name, it would be hard to track down them and their descendants. But there appeared to be a partial code. Rosalind Widdick had become Rosalind Touhy, and Richard Widdick was supposed to be Richard Hardy. First names probably stayed the same.

"Who are the trustees of the foundation?" I asked.

She gave me five names. One was Anthony Broadmead, and I realized with a start that he must be my grandson. Another was Robert Hawkins. Hah!

Make it Robert Widdick. I didn't bother to ask. The other names were William Ferrante, Joseph Moody, and Miranda Moley. I would have bet my soul, so nearly lost already, that they were really Widdicks.

While we were in flight Roz described my fictitious past as Richard Hardy, now age twenty-five. "You should memorize this," she said, giving me a packet of information supposedly about myself. "You are now a graduate student at Cornell, with a fellowship from New World Enterprises, and my husband is your faculty adviser."

I inspected a birth certificate, school and college transcripts, and other records, even photographs. "Fantastic!" I exclaimed. "Who arranged all this?"

She brushed the question aside by answering, "A committee." Then she handed me a plastic card like a credit card. "This is your UC, your universal card. It has your Social Security number, your credit number for everything from hamburgers to phone calls to flier rentals, and your medical history number. Stick it in a slot, and a computer does the rest." She laughed. "We have been using it on your behalf, building up a history, for twenty years."

"What is supposed to have happened to Richard Widdick?"

"He died today."

I would have to be very patient, very cautious, to unravel a deception so elaborate if I was going to expose it.

In my newly found patience and caution, life with the Touhy family went smoothly. Rosalind's husband knew about me and didn't ask questions. The children, Malcolm and Marian, were at school during the day. I listened to them prattle at suppertime and pictured them burning in Hell.

"What happened to your arm?" Malcolm asked the first time he saw my stump.

"I lost it in a war long ago."

"Why don't you get a new one?" Marian asked.

"It's a badge of honor, like a medal." Also, I had thought of a way that my stump could be valuable.

I read and wrote about the influence of Calvinist thought upon economics. I prayed. And I listened to Roz, toured the area with her, and learned to let computers and robots tend my needs.

At first Roz watched me carefully, more an observer, even a guard, than a sister who was hostess and teacher, but gradually she warmed toward me. She was always glad to talk about her genetic research and her abominable ability to make changes in God's design.

She explained the accident that had put the R-factor gene on one of her X-chromosomes. "We can clone the gene now for both men and women," she said. "It can't change them into people like us because we can't insert the gene into a chromosome in a newly fertilized zygote before the cells start to divide. Later on we could uses viruses containing the gene to infect the cells of the body with it, but there are too many cells, trillions of them. We tried it with animals, and it doesn't work."

Infection was the right word. The R-factor was a disease like other inherited diseases. I was glad she had failed.

"The Bureau of Genetic Standards monitors our research," Roz told me. "The use of cloned genes is very carefully regulated."

In the summer of 2085 Roz and her family took me with them to a private resort beside a lake in Minnesota. "It's time to meet your cousins," she said. "Remember, some of them have the R-factor and some don't, so we don't talk about it."

There must have been a hundred men, women, and children at the lake. They swam, fished, and sailed, and they played baseball, soccer, volleyball, and baseball, all wasting time happily, with thoughtless outcries of joy from the children. The older ones played underwater tag in the lake with jet-assisted scuba-diving gear. I remembered sinfully skimpy bathing suits from the past, but the topless suits that adolescent girls wore now approached utter depravity.

Many of the names were not Widdick. Some of them would be descended from daughters who did not have the R-factor. This made it hard for me to determine who did have it. If a man was over sixty, I could rule out anyone who had his last name, because he would not be the son of a Yf man.

Or almost rule him out. "The R-Phase doesn't drop on Yf men like a brick on their sixtieth birthday," Roz told me. "It happens sometime during that year, but there is a little variation. And then he lives to sixty-two before his second R-Phase starts."

The man I wanted to see was my father, who now, if I was right, called himself Robert Hawkins. Three days after my arrival I was swimming, avoiding the Sodom and Gomorrah elsewhere on the lake, when I saw a flier land. A message came: "Please see Robert at the lodge."

He was sitting in a wicker chair on the veranda, recognizable at once, even without the beard I remembered. He rose to shake my hand and said, "I'm glad to see you, Dick. Roz tells me you're not the firebrand you used to be. How do you feel about the R-factor these days?"

I was careful not to pretend that I had completely discarded old convictions. "I still don't like it," I said, "but since I've come out of an R-Phase I've been thinking things through again."

"Having the experience yourself makes a difference, doesn't it? Usually it's hard at first because of all you've forgotten, but then you make a new life for yourself." He waved at mixed teams of boys and girls playing baseball on a field in front of us. "Half of them have the R and half don't. I defy anyone to tell the difference. We are like anyone else. I'm glad I have a chance to see my descendants. I'm proud of all of them."

"How many of them have the R-factor?" I asked.

"Forty-six, including five boys born in the last four years. There were two more, but they died. One drowned as a child. The other was killed thirteen years ago when a large rock struck his ship in space on a trip to Mars Colony."

"I'm sorry," I said.

"Why?" Robert asked sharply. "You never heard of him before this minute."

I realized that I was on probation. "He was a member of the family."

Satisfied, he nodded. "I see you understand the importance of our survival."

"But why do people in the N-Phase take new names?"

"Protective coloration. They don't have to answer a lot of questions."

Obviously that wasn't the whole answer, but I let it pass. "Where is the clinic that took care of me in my R-Phase?"

"There is a lot you will learn in time. I'm more interested in you. What do you want to do? The degree you're getting doesn't matter. You can get just about any kind of work with one of our companies."

He had adopted a pose of friendly interest, but his evading an answer to my question about the clinic showed that he didn't trust me. My own pose would have to be one of gradual conversion to belief that the R-factor was good. And cooperation with Robert's plans. I had thought about a cover job, so now I said, "You must have an advertising department. Maybe I could fit in there. I used to be good at art."

He frowned, obviously remembering the scenes of Hell I had painted, but he said, "There's plenty of time to make up your mind. Relax while you're here and get acquainted. Do you see that eighteen-year-old boy playing first base? He's your new half-brother, Vernon, Becky's and my son."

Another blight upon humanity, I thought. More disturbing, because I had to blame myself, was the presence of two grandsons, both about twice my apparent age, and a great-grandson. The last, Ben Widdick, was twenty-five, only a year younger than I seemed. I avoided all three of them. I began to wonder if the family curse had spread too widely for me to combat it. I could not foresee the opportunity that was to come.

By saying little but listening carefully, I had sorted out most of the family, including those with assumed names, by the end of the vacation at the lake. Two more interesting things happened that summer.

One day Miranda Bannister Moley arrived in a flier to pick up Rosalind. "We're going to see Julia in the clinic," Roz told me. I understood by now that Miranda was the daughter of the Julia McVeigh Bannister I had met in the clinic, but I didn't know Roz's connection. After she had gone, I asked her husband.

"She's Julia's mother," Professor Touhy answered with surprise. "Didn't you know that? Her first time around Roz married a doctor named McVeigh. She had two daughters, Julia and Portia. She hardly knows Julia."

He got a paper and pencil, still useful in this age of computers, and made some calculations. "Julia was born in 2017. She entered the R-Phase in 2069, the same year Roz came out of it. But Roz's memory had gone back to the year 2009, when she was twenty-two, years before the girls were born. Sometimes it drives her glitch not to know her own daughter. She talks to Julia at the clinic to store memories second hand. Right now Julia thinks she's in the year 2045. Roz knows it's useless in the long run. If the cycles keep their schedule, Julia will come out of R in 2099, and Roz will go into it again two years later and start forgetting everything."

"How do Julia and her daughter Miranda fit the picture?" I asked.

"They'll be out of phase, too, although not as much because Julia had her children when she was younger. Miranda doesn't like to watch her mother's regression and know it will happen to her. But Roz is the one who really gets depressed. She aches at the gaps left by loss of memory. I tell you, I would rather lose an arm." He looked at my stump and said, "Oh. Sorry. Anyway, I'm glad I'll take my memories with me when I go. I won't know the difference."

Questions filled my mind. First I asked, "What happened to Roz's other daughter, Portia?"

"She's growing old, like most people, and getting a little dotty. She's sixty-five now. A boy can't help but inherit the R if his father has it, but a girl has a fifty-fifty chance of inheriting the X-chromosome with the R or the one without it. That bothers Roz, too."

Next question: "How do you feel about freaks like Roz and me?"

"You can speak for yourself," he said dryly, "but Roz is no freak. She's a fine woman. I might add that both of our children have the R, and they're not freaks."

"How can a boy get the R from his mother?" I asked with surprise.

"He inherits an X-chromosome from her, doesn't he? It's fifty-fifty that he'll get the one with the Xf gene. Julia was the first to pass the R on to a son. You must know by now that she has a son, Fred, as well as her daughter, Miranda. Genetically Fred is the first XfY male. His daughter got the X with an R from him, but his son got an ordinary Y."

Luckily for him, I thought. "And the children of Miranda Bannister Moley?" I found it easier to keep the women straight if I used their maiden names as well as their married names.

"Her daughter has R but her son doesn't. With odds of fifty-fifty, half the people lose and half win. I won't say which group is the winner here."

I wrote down the possible combinations of sex chromosomes to make sure I had them straight. Start with two ordinary Xs from a mother and either an X or a Y from a father.

1. X or X with X or Y gave four possible combinations: XX, XX, XY, XY. Neither sons nor daughters had R.

2. XX with XYf gave XX, XX, XYf, XYf. All sons had R, but no daughters had it.

3. XfX with XY gave XfX, XX, XfY, XY. Half of the daughters and half of the sons would have R.

4. XX with XfY gave XXf, XXf, XY, XY. All of the daughters but none of the sons would have R.

A son could inherit R from his mother, as in formula 3, but could pass it on only to daughters.

I felt that I was missing something. Whatever it was, the thought eluded me.

Then I discovered that I had grown too proud of my power to deceive the family, and incautious. My comeuppance came at a party for William Ferrante. He was sixty-two, about to enter the R-Phase for the second time. Others who had been through it gathered to wish him well. I had no personal recollection of him, except for meeting him at the summer resort, but I assumed that he had been born a Widdick, emerging from his first R-Phase to take the name Ferrante.

They all took aliases! I was furious. Because men changed their names and women changed theirs twice, first when they married and again when they came out of R, keeping track of those who carried the curse would become harder and harder.

Robert "Hawkins," as the one who had been out of R the longest, since 2059, was host. Other celebrants were Joseph "Moody," Alfred "Graham," David "Mitchell," my sister Rosalind "Touhy," and myself, Richard "Hardy."

They invited me because they think I am one of them, I thought resentfully. William clapped me on the shoulder when I entered with Roz and said, "It's good to see you, Dick. It's encouraging to see a man the age I will reach once again. I hate to think of living in limbo for thirty-seven years, but the reward will be waiting at the end of it."

"Reward!" I burst out. "It's punishment. I must live with full knowledge of my sin!"

The others fell silent. Finally Robert said softly, "So you still feel that way."

"So should you all!" Nothing could stop me as pent-up feelings broke the dam of caution. "We are all damned! The least we could do to lessen our sin is to stop having children, stop spreading the curse, but what do you all do? When you recover your youth, you marry and breed again. You are instruments of Satan!"

"Have a good day, as they used to say in 1978, the first time I was twenty-five," William said with hostile mockery.

"This is serious," Robert said, reproving him. "I thought you had come to like the rest of the family, Dick. They live useful lives and harm no one. The world is a better place for their being here. We set standards of decency and public service. Our companies make useful products. Our genetic research alone has led to cures for most illnesses."

"And made you rich," I answered.

"Nevertheless, the people who recover are grateful," Robert said. "You forget something else. People who live more than once take a very long view. Who has done as much as we have to promote the preservation of nature and an end to pollution? Most people are more concerned about their own comfort and convenience than about what their grandchildren will face. We will be there with our grandchildren. We work on reforestation and more sophisticated means of restoring the earth's climate to what it once was, not as hot and dry, with more fertile land."

"Your ends do not justify your means," I said. "Salvation is not found on this earth."

"If you feel so strongly, what do you plan to do?"

Suddenly I realized that I had gone too far. My masquerade was exposed. I did not yet know all I needed to know, and I had no plan. "I don't know," I answered. "I suppose I'll go ahead and design advertising layouts to sell fancy hormones. But I won't have more children. And I won't stay here to celebrate an abomination!"

I ordered a public flier, which landed under robot control, and returned to the Touhy house.

Roz was relieved when I left soon afterwards. I took my low-level job in the advertising department of New World Technology and found a cubbyhole for rent that I could afford. During my free time I reconstructed the past that I had forgotten.

It was easy. The unlimited memory of computers and easy retrieval of what is stored has encouraged the pack rat mentality of the human race to keep records of everything. I paid for searches of what was known about Richard Widdick and found newspaper clippings and videotapes that included a report of my "death" two years earlier, in 2084. There was more than I had expected for the years from when I lost my arm in the war until 2049, when I disappeared from public view. I discovered with pleasure that I had become a leading Tri-D evangelist with my Church of Sinners Repentant. I had preached against the Widdick curse and had berated the Bureau of Genetic Standards for ignoring it.

I had done my duty, but to what avail?

The church still existed, although the sermons showed that it had forgotten about the Widdicks. I attended, discreetly, and concluded that I could use it again at the right time.

Where I failed was in searching for records of the R-factor. Perhaps the Bureau had them, but its files were confidential.

But I knew the names of those who had entered the R-Phase and the names they had taken on returning to an N-Phase. Besides those who had been at the party for William Ferrante, there were those I had met in my last days at the clinic, Harry Solway, Julia McVeigh Bannister, James Duval, my son Philip Broadmead, and five men named Widdick. I searched civic records of marriages and births, no matter where they had taken place.

I had to put myself on a starvation diet to save money to pay for it all, but in the end I was sure I had a complete reconstruction of the family tree stemming from Robert Widdick.

I was ready to act when Divine Providence granted my chance.

Chapter Seven

The first serious trouble for the family did not come from Richard, but we can imagine him getting on his knees to give thanks when he heard about it. He had not had to wait long for his opportunity, and he wasted no time taking advantage of it. One woman's resentment, superstition, and tempest of insanity, combined with Richard's permanent derangement and stubborn vindictiveness, brought the R-factor out of the shadows. It also brought into play qualities quite different from Robert's usual method of planning his moves before making them, like a chess player. He had to react to the unexpected.

—GABRIEL (D) CHEN, ARCHIVIST

Flushed Out
By Robert (C) Hawkins (2087)

On August 7 last year, Rupert called and told me that Portia had stabbed Julia. Next morning the pub-

lic learned about it from the *Juniper County News*.
A fax of the newspaper story follows:

Woman stabs sister,
calls her a witch

A woman botanist was charged yesterday
with trying to kill her sister, whom she called
a witch.

Portia McVeigh, 67, allegedly stabbed her
sister, Julia McVeigh Bannister, 69, who is a
patient at a private clinic for amnesiacs, with
a paring knife. Bannister suffered a punctured
lung but is expected to recover.

A nurse, Luisa Pedrano, described the incident to police.

"I was in the dayroom when McVeigh came
to visit Bannister," police said Pedrano told
them. "I heard McVeigh scream, 'Witch!' at
her sister and saw her pull a knife from her
purse and stab her in the side.

"Two men patients wrestled the knife away
and held McVeigh. She was hysterical. She
kept screaming, 'She's a witch! She's a
witch!' and struggling to break free and
hit her."

The clinic, the Juniper Treatment Facility,
is seven miles from Juniper Falls. The director, Dr. Rupert Solway, gave emergency aid
to Bannister and injected a sedative in the
arm of McVeigh. Accompanied by Pedrano,
he flew the sisters to Juniper Falls Hospital
in an ambulance.

Solway committed McVeigh to the psychiatric ward of the hospital for observation.
Hospital authorities called police to investigate
the stabbing.

Bannister could not be questioned because

she was in the intensive care unit, and McVeigh was still under sedation.

"Miss McVeigh was temporarily distraught," Solway told police. "I think the whole thing can be forgotten. Mrs. Bannister will suffer no permanent harm."

Police, however, filed a charge of attempted murder pending further investigation.

"The police showed up last night," Rupert told me when I called him after reading the story. He looked grim and exhausted on the phone screen. "They found the knife, which still had blood on it, in a wastebasket where somebody threw it. None of the patients, of course, remembered the incident. I hadn't seen it because I was in my office until I heard the commotion in the dayroom. Luisa Pedrano is the only witness."

With the victim and the weapon, one witness was enough, I thought. That wasn't what worried me. I asked Rupert how long Pedrano had been a nurse at the clinic.

"Six months," he said.

"Then she hasn't been there long enough to watch anyone grow younger."

"No, but she saw that Julia looks more like Portia's daughter than her sister."

"Give her a bonus for help in an emergency and tell her to keep her mouth shut."

Portia worried me more. Not having an R-gene herself, she had not been told about it, but in paying occasional duty calls on her sister in the clinic, she had watched Julia grow younger. People wouldn't pay much attention to a sisterly squabble that led to a nonfatal stabbing, but a charge of witchcraft was juicy stuff. People would want to know more.

I called my great-grandson Alfred, who is using the name Graham in his second N-Phase. He is president of New World Resources, which employs Portia as an expert on reforestation, and is a trustee of the foundation. "Find a lawyer, not someone in the family, to get your loyal employee out of the hospital and keep her out of jail," I told him. "Send her on a job that will keep her in cold storage, off in the wilds somewhere."

"Portia is too old for field work," Alfred said.

"Baloney. I've seen people in their eighties plant seedlings or take a census of caterpillars."

"I'll have her make a fungus survey. She's big on fungus."

I also called Roz. After all, she was the mother of Julia and Portia. "I heard about it," she told me. "Video gave us a bite on the witchcraft angle."

"I can't think of anything you can do," I said. "Julia will recover. Portia doesn't know about your N-Phase and thinks you died years ago."

"If I show up, she'll call me a witch, too."

I laughed and said, "What you stir in a flask entitles you to a broomstick."

The lawyer got Portia freed on a token bond of $100,000 at the preliminary hearing on the charge of attempted murder. New World Resources put up the money. After the judge rejected a motion to dismiss the case, the lawyer entered pleas of not guilty and not guilty by reason of insanity. The latter plea enraged Portia, who talked to a reporter after the hearing.

"I'm not crazy!" the reporter's story quoted her. "My sister is sixty-nine years old, but look at her. She looks thirty-five. Only a witch would grow younger again. The world should be rid of her kind."

Alfred chased her off to northern Maine on a fungus survey before anyone else could talk to her.

And then I discovered what a mess we were in. An anonymous letter urged me to watch a program on the Evangelical Network "which will be of great personal interest." A private gumshoe agency had been keeping track of my mulish son Richard for me, and I suspected that he would be involved.

The video show began with a camera panning across a church congregation before it zoomed in on a choir singing. Voice-over: "Today, on the anniversary of the founding of the Church of Sinners Repentant sixty-six years ago, the first prophet of the church has promised that the founding prophet, Richard Widdick, will return."

Oh, my God, I thought. He's using his original name, not Richard Hardy. I watched file clips of Richard preaching, brandishing the stump of his upper left arm, as the voice said: "This is Richard Widdick, prominent evangelist of the thirties and forties. And now the first prophet is coming to the altar."

Files of hooded men and women came down the center aisle, men on the right, in white, women on the left, in red. As they turned to stand on both sides of the altar, a man wearing a white robe trimmed in gold, his head bare, ended the procession. He took his place behind the altar and raised both arms.

Close-up of first prophet. "Salvation to the faithful!"

Congregation shouts, "Salvation!"

First prophet: "Today a miracle is granted! Our blessed founding prophet, Richard Widdick, has returned to us. His youth has been renewed for him to strive again mightily for the salvation of our souls! Bear witness to his coming!"

A man in a black robe and black cowl walks slowly down the aisle. Congregation murmurs. Some stand for a better look. Man goes behind altar, where first prophet makes way for him. Man stands quietly. Congregation grows hushed. Close-up as man throws cowl off his head, back to his shoulders, to show his blond hair and stern young face. He lifts the stump of his left arm. Large screens above and to both sides of altar show tapes of Richard Widdick preaching, in the same pose, fifty years earlier. It is clearly the same Richard Widdick who has returned. An excited babble from the congregation can be heard.

Widdick: "Repent!"

Congregation, on its feet, chants a response: "Repent and be saved!"

As if on cue, somebody shouts, "Messiah!"

Back to Widdick. He raises his right arm with his hand out to quiet everyone. "I am no messiah. I am a miserable sinner. My soul is blacker than my clothing." He brandishes his stump. "I bear forever this badge of shame."

Pause. Camera remains locked on Widdick.

Widdick: "You see me as a man in his twenties. This semblance is a mockery, a curse! I was born ninety-seven years ago! I have lived well past the span allotted by the Lord. Thus have I sinned, and I have compounded this sin almost beyond hope by growing young again. Yet we must never abandon hope in the mercy of the Lord. My hope is that I can atone for my sin by preaching words of truth and faith. The first truth I bring to you is that others besides myself are living a second life, and even a third!"

Full of apprehension, I waited as he continued:

"I live again because my flesh is corrupt. Their flesh is corrupt. The flesh of their children and grandchildren is corrupt! The corruption spreads among us! Satan has tricked us into turning our hearts away from heavenly salvation by the temptation of repeated lives. I tell you that salvation is not to be found in mortal life!

"In days to come I will reveal to you who these people are who spread this corruption—oh, very secretly!—among us. At the proper time I will reveal everything about their conspiracy of sin. Pray for me!"

If he wants to expose us, I thought angrily, what's he waiting for? He wants the congregation to accept him for what he says he is first, and he wants a brush fire of curiosity and suspense to spread. I wondered how many lies it would take to keep the R-factor hidden, and what we should do if we failed.

A man who identified himself as a reporter for the "Oboto Show" called to ask if the Health Research Foundation operated the Juniper Treatment Facility.

"I'll have to look it up," I answered, stalling. "We have a couple hundred operations. Why do you ask?"

"I want to know if Dr. Peter Widdick is a patient there."

"Why don't you ask at the facility?"

"I did. The doctor in charge said he could not give out any information."

The doctor would be Julia's son, Fred Bannister, I thought. Rupert Solway had entered the R-Phase a month after the stabbing, conveniently removing himself as a witness as he joined his former wards.

"That sounds like normal concern for a patient's privacy," I said.

"Mr. Oboto likes confirmation from other sources of information he has received."

Why would Peter, who had been my doctor before I came out of R in 2059 and he entered it in 2065, interest a video personality so many years later, in 2086? "What's this all about?" I asked.

"You'll have to watch the show for that, Mr. Hawkins."

I watched. Indeed I did. I sat through a commercial for Wufflies, 'Everybody's Breakfast Dumpling,' which I detested, to be sure not to miss the beginning of the show. I eat oatmeal, which is hard to find these days. I had to buy a mill to be sure of a supply.

Medium close-up of Oboto, who does not use a first name, at a desk. A clean-shaven man the color of coffee with two spoons of whitish. Red T-shirt, yellow jacket with spangles. A globe spins slowly on the desk. Voice-over: "No corner of the world is hidden from Oboto."

Oboto smiles. "How true. But sometimes the strangest corners are in our own back yard. Have you seen a witch lately? Portia McVeigh believes she has."

Portia's picture, thin face, gray hair, appears on a screen to Oboto's right. "Portia McVeigh is sixty-seven years old. A sweet lady, too busy working for the survival of our planet"—Oboto spins the globe—"to be with us tonight. Portia McVeigh is free on bond on a charge of trying to kill her sister. She told police her sister is a witch."

Screen beside Oboto splits to show Portia's picture on one side and the face of a dark-haired woman, in a dressing gown, beside it. "Can you guess who that is? How old do you think she is? The picture was taken last month. Come, guess her age."

Camera shows audience, row on row. "Forty!" a woman shouts. "Thirty-two!" shouts a man. So many people begin shouting that it's hard to distinguish one guess from another.

Oboto: "She is sixty-nine years old. That is Julia McVeigh Bannister, Portia McVeigh's sister, whom Portia is accused of stabbing. The picture was taken last month by an employee of Juniper Falls Hospital, where Julia was recovering from a severe knife wound in her side."

Damn whoever took, and sold, that picture, I thought.

Oboto: "Portia McVeigh told police her sister was growing younger. You be the judges of that. Portia said her sister was a witch." Pause for effect. "I will show you one more picture."

Group shot appears on screen above the other one. "This was taken during a vacation more than thirty years ago, in 2052." Two of the faces, indistinct among others, zoom forward, enlarged. "On the left is Portia McVeigh, then thirty-three years old. How time wounds us all! Or nearly all. On the right is Julia McVeigh Bannister, who was thirty-five. She looks much as she does this year, doesn't she?"

The blowups up of Portia and Julia recede. Two more faces are brought forward, enlarged. "Those are Dr. Peter Widdick and his wife, Bella. Bella is with us tonight."

Sandbagged, I thought.

Cut to close-up of Bella Widdick, wrinkled face, tinted blond hair, glasses, bunched forward in a chair.

Oboto: "Why are you here tonight, Mrs. Widdick?"

"I'm a friend of Portia McVeigh. People say she's crazy, but she isn't. Julia is growing younger. So are other people."

"How do you know that?"

"Because I watched my husband grow younger. He was a doctor in the clinic where it happens, and then it happened to him."

Screen splits to show Oboto on one side, Bella Widdick on the other, as interview continues.

"Do they practice witchcraft in this clinic, Mrs. Widdick?"

Shrill laugh. "No. Growing younger is born in them. They have a gene called the R-factor. My husband told me all about it. They slide into amnesia at a certain age and forget more and more as they grow younger."

"How long does this go on?"

"Until they're back in their twenties again. Then they take new names and start new lives."

Oboto's mouth drops open in simulated amazement. "Do you mean they live again and again?"

"I don't know if it happens more than once."

"Do you know anyone it's happened to at all?"

"I'm not sure. How can you tell, with the new names? That family group you showed a picture of, we were all supposed to be cousins or married to cousins. A lot of them were named Widdick, but there were different names."

"What is the name of the clinic where people grow younger?"

"The Juniper Treatment Facility, near Juniper Falls, in upstate New York."

Oboto faces audience. "That's where Portia McVeigh is said to have stabbed her sister." Faces Bella. "Who runs it?"

"Peter told me it was set up by the Health Research Foundation."

Oboto faces audience again. "I feel compelled to point out that both Dr. Fred Bannister, who is in charge of the clinic, and Robert Hawkins, who is present of the Health Research Foundation, refused to answer questions by my staff. The Health Research Foundation is a private foundation that owns New World Technology and many profitable companies. Friends, they have plenty of money to run a small, private clinic."

Well. It was out. All except the new names taken in the N-Phase, and we hadn't yet heard from my son Richard. I had to answer a lot of questions from the media.

"The clinic is for amnesiacs," I said. "The patients may appear to grow younger, but our records show that they die." It wasn't a lie. That's what the records showed. "The treatment facility is a very small operation, a branch of our research hospital. Yes, the amnesia, which is a serious disability, is caused by a gene, the R-factor. It is on record with the Bureau of Genetic Standards."

I had tried to make the point that the R-factor was a disadvantage, not a benefit, and to suggest that BGS knew all about it.

The board met to discuss what to do.

Anthony Broadmead, Richard's grandson, was now fifty-six, an engineer who had moved from the space program to become president of New World

Technology. "I would hate to see the fallout from this hurt our reputation," he said. "We're coming out with a new household control center, and we have tough competition."

Joseph, who was forty-three in his N-Phase as Joseph Moody, was in charge of public relations and lobbying. "Beef up your ads a bit. You'll be all right. What we have to worry about is the foundation itself and what it's done for us. A lot of poor people will be hostile to rich people who get free care in a private clinic. And they will envy second lives because they would like a second chance. I suggest a low-key public relations program emphasizing the medical benefits from foundation research, and about the free clinics."

We agreed on that. Whatever happened, we could hope to have public opinion in our favor.

"We may need something more dramatic," Miranda said. She is Julia's daughter, Miranda Bannister Moley. Now forty-six, she headed a department of the Bureau of Genetic Standards. "How is Roz's project coming? She hasn't told the bureau a word about it."

"She's about ready to go," I answered.

"It might be helpful if she could speed it up."

"Maybe we should move the clinic," Alfred said. "Someplace really out of sight, like the Maine forests, or even Canada."

An intense feeling of rebellion against the forces closing in on us came over me. "I won't spend my life, and my next phase if I have one, running away," I said emphatically. I was fifty-two now, for the third time. "We have nothing to be ashamed of. Our best defense against whatever Richard dumps on us is the truth, although as little as we can get away with. If he can show that I am really Robert Widdick, going under the name of Robert Hawkins, I will admit it. I will concede that others are using aliases for renewed lives, but I won't say who they are. None of us has broken any laws. We have not collected life insurance, because we don't have any. We have stopped collecting Medicare at the dates of our supposed deaths. We have not committed bigamy, because we divorce our wives." I looked at Miranda. "Or husbands. An audit will show that no federal funds are going to the clinic."

Joseph grinned when I subsided. "Sounds great. But we have developed nepotism, special favors to members of the family, to a degree that beats a royal dynasty. We have created an exclusive class of people."

"Necessary under the circumstances," I snapped. "Get on with your PR job while we wait for Richard to stomp his boot in our faces."

I took the blame for Richard's learning enough to hurt us. A normal father never gives up hope that a son who has gone astray will come to his senses, but I didn't even have that feeling for him. During my second R-Phase I forgot his existence, and when I went into N again, I knew about him only from reading about him. I suppose that I took a chance on bringing him back into the family because I hoped to hold the family together.

Roz may be in trouble on this, I thought, because I persuaded her to give him his new ID and to baby him along. I flew to Ithaca and told her how I saw her situation. "You can tell people I gave you the packet for Dick," I said. "You don't know where I got it."

"Fine, but what do I say when he says I'm his

sister and your daughter and I went through the R-Phase to start a new life?"

"Call him a liar. You have documentation. No; that won't work. People would ask why I turned him over to you. Maybe you could get away with no comment."

"That won't work either."

"I suppose not," I said. "How's your project?"

"I'm on the final tests."

"We may need to announce the results soon."

Richard was tormenting me by his inaction. He preached hellfire and damnation, standard stuff, but it won an ever larger following. He gave evidence that he was indeed the original Richard Widdick, born ninety-seven years earlier. His fingerprints from army service were still on file under the government theory that files are written in gold. His present fingerprints matched. For those who understood genetics, he had a gene map made, and he obtained from the Bureau of Genetic Standards, as he was authorized to do, an identical map, made fifty-one years earlier by the Bureau. But he gave no more details about his revival than he had in his first appearance as the founding prophet who had returned.

Alfred called to tell me that Portia had been summoned back from the woods to go on trial. "Her lawyer tells me that the district attorney will attack her defense of temporary insanity by trying to prove she was sane. Her sister, Julia, was growing younger, as Portia said. The DA's witnesses include Richard."

"And he saw Julia in the hospital," I observed.

"He can testify that Portia had reason to believe that people grow younger in the clinic. Therefore, the DA will argue, she was not insane. She was not temporarily insane because her action in stabbing Julia was not spontaneous. It was planned, as shown by her bringing a knife to the clinic with her. The planning is what makes it attempted murder."

"But Portia talked about witchcraft. That makes her insane. It seems to me that Richard's testimony is immaterial and should not be allowed."

"That's what Portia's lawyer will argue. It will be tricky."

Roz called to say that she was going to go to a conference in Copenhagen before the trial began and then tour genetics laboratories abroad. "I can't bear to watch one daughter on trial for stabbing another," she said.

"Also, you might be dragged in as a witness on Richard's claims."

I didn't attend the trial either. I could imagine Richard rising to his feet from the witness chair, pointing at me, and shouting, "And there he is! The man who started it all!" Then I would be called to the stand. I didn't have to attend. The idea that people could grow younger had become so exciting to the public that the trial received live Tri-D coverage.

While Julia was in the hospital, the police had compared her blood with blood on the knife and found them identical. The district attorney had succeeded in interviewing her at the treatment facility and had discovered that she didn't remember the stabbing. But the nurse did, and the hospital had records on Julia, including pictures of her wound, and the D.A. could produce the weapon. There was no doubt that the stabbing had occurred. Whether it was attempted murder would have to be argued.

Now the D.A. attempted to demolish the defense of temporary insanity. His line was that Portia had reason to believe in witchcraft because she had watched her sister and others grow younger and had no other explanation. He called to the stand Bella Widdick, Peter's wife, who had appeared on the "Oboto Show."

D.A.: "When did you last see your husband? Mrs. Widdick."

Bella: "Eleven years ago, in 2075."

D.A.: "Where did you see him?"

Bella: "In the Juniper Treatment Facility near Juniper Falls, New York."

"Were you married to him at the time?"

"No, we were divorced when he became a patient with amnesia in 2065, but I was still fond of him and called on him over the years."

"How did he appear to you in 2075?"

"Well, his amnesia was worse. He wasn't sure who I was. He was seventy now, but he looked about fifty, and I had become sixty-seven. He remembered things until the year he was fifty. He thought of one of our grandchildren, who was a grown man, as a baby, and he didn't remember the other one at all."

"That was eleven years ago. Why haven't you seen him since?"

"Because I knew it would grow worse. He would lose more and more of his memory as he kept growing younger. And I didn't want to be an old woman and have him see me that way when he was young again."

"What made you think this would happen?"

"Peter had told me. He said men in his family had a gene called the R-factor that made them lose their memories and grow younger until they were twenty-five again and could start a new life."

"Did you see anyone else who seemed to be growing younger?"

"Yes. There were some cousins I watched grow younger over the years. I knew two of them, Leo and George Widdick, well. There was also a man named Harry Solway, whom I had met years earlier. He had looked like he was in his sixties then, but now he seemed to be in his forties."

"His name was not Harry Widdick?"

"No. Harry Solway."

"Did your husband tell you that the R-factor gene ran only in the family or that other people had it, too?"

"He said he never heard of it except in the family."

"Did your husband tell you how men who come out of amnesia as younger men start a new life?"

"He said they take new names. He said he would call himself Peter Smith. He said the Health Research Foundation, which runs the clinic, helped them get started."

"Tell me, Mrs. Widdick, did you see Julia McVeigh Bannister on your visit to the clinic in 2075?"

"Yes."

"How did she appear to you?"

"I don't remember anything special. She had gone into the clinic only six years earlier, when she was fifty-two, and I didn't notice a change."

The district attorney didn't think to ask Bella whether Peter had told her that women could inherit the R-factor. Defense counsel let that question lie. It came up when Richard testified, as I had been told he would do.

Richard smiled confidently at the jury as he walked to the stand. He strutted, swinging his stump of an arm, shoulders back and head high, a man whose handsome face was known by now to millions who had watched him preach on video. Defense counsel had made sure that no members of Richard's church, and no fundamentalists at all, were accepted for the jury. Meanwhile the district attorney had rejected people with a scientific or technical background. Everyone on the jury had an elementary knowledge of genes and chromosomes, as everyone does these days, but their knowledge was vague. They had low- to moderate-income jobs or none at all. The defense attorney had tried to keep elderly, retired people off the jury but had run out of challenges.

D.A.: "Will you please identify yourself."

Richard: "I am the Reverend Dr. Richard Widdick, the founding prophet of the Church of Sinners Repentant."

D.A.: "How old are you?"

Richard: "I am ninety-seven years old. I was born in 1989."

"Do you realize that you look like a man in his twenties?"

With a grin, "I do. I am now twenty-seven years old."

Somebody laughed, and the judge banged his gavel.

D.A. to Richard: "Which are you, ninety-seven or twenty-seven?"

"I have lived for ninety-seven years, but when I was sixty, in the year 2049, I entered a clinic and grew younger over the next thirty-five years. When

I came out of the clinic two years ago, I was twenty-five again."

Murmurs from the audience.

"Was Julia McVeigh Bannister a patient in this clinic?"

"She was."

"Did she grow younger?"

"I believe so, but I had a form of amnesia that prevented me from remembering her or what she might have looked like in the past."

Defense attorney: "Objection, your honor. The witness does not remember Julia McVeigh Bannister. Move to strike that testimony."

Judge: "Sustained. The last question and answer about Julia McVeigh Bannister will be stricken from the testimony."

Richard looked angry. The district attorney did not ask him about others who might have grown younger in the clinic. He changed his tack.

D.A.: "Can you prove that you were born in 1989?"

Richard: "I can. I have my birth certificate and army records, and my fingerprints from my right hand"—he held out both his right hand and the stump of his left arm—"and blood tests and my gene map show I'm the same person."

"When, as you say, you became twenty-five again, did you continue to use the name Richard Widdick?"

"Not at first. I used the name Richard Hardy."

"Why did you do that?"

"Because there's a conspiracy—"

Defense counsel: "Objection! I request that the witness be directed to confine his answers to his own actions and omit speculation."

Judge: "So ordered."

D.A.: "Why did you use the name Richard Hardy, Dr. Widdick?"

Richard: "Because when I got out of the clinic, I was met by my sister, Rosalind, who told me my name was Richard Hardy and gave me a packet of materials documenting my supposed life for the past twenty-five years. There was a fraudulent birth certificate. There was even a newspaper clipping reporting that I had lost my arm, not in the war, as I had, but in a chain saw accident."

"What is your sister's full name?"

"Today it's Rosalind Harper Touhy. It used to be Rosalind Widdick McVeigh. She told me she took the name Harper after she had gone through amnesia and started a second life, and then she married Professor Touhy. She told me we all take new names."

"Is your sister related to Portia McVeigh and Julia McVeigh Bannister?"

"Yes. She's their mother."

The crowd in the courtroom, which had listened, hushed, to the testimony, murmured at the thought that this young man's sister could be the mother of women in their sixties. Richard explained that Roz had been born ninety-nine years ago but now appeared to be in her thirties. Richard hadn't said so in so many words, but the Bureau of Genetic Standards would be quick to understand what it hadn't known before, that women could inherit the R-factor. The secret was out.

D.A.: "Is your sister present in this courtroom?"

Richard, after looking around: "No, she's not."

"Did your sister tell you where she got the documentation for your life under a new name?"

"She said it was prepared by a committee set up by the Health Research Foundation."

"What can you tell us about the foundation?"

"It was set up by my father, Robert Widdick, about a hundred years ago to hold family assets, receive income from them, and spend the income. I don't know what all the assets are, but New World Technology is one of them."

"Besides yourself and your sister, have you seen anyone else grow younger?"

"About fifteen of them."

More murmurs from the audience.

D.A.: "Have you, personally, watched this happen?"

Richard: "Well, no. I know about them, like I know about Portia Bannister, but I have watched it with only one of them."

"And who is that?"

"My father, Robert Widdick. He uses the name Robert Hawkins now. He is chairman of the Health Research Foundation."

That was it. My secret had become public knowledge.

D.A.: "How do you know he has grown younger?"

Richard: "I saw him last year. He looked the same age as when I saw him the last time I was a young man, more than seventy years ago." Suddenly Richard shouted. "And this isn't the first time! He's living his third life now! When I was a boy he admitted he had lived before. He told me about the R-factor gene that causes it and said it would happen to me, too. I didn't want to. It's a sin! Robert Widdick brought a new temptation from the devil into this world, and it's spreading!"

The district attorney saw that Richard was winding up for a sermon and said quickly, "Do you believe in witchcraft, Dr. Widdick?"

Richard: "Of course I do. It's in the Bible. Exodus 22 says, 'Thou shalt not suffer a witch to live.' First Samuel 28 tells how Saul consulted the Witch of Endor."

"Do you believe that witchcraft makes people grow younger at the Juniper Treatment Facility?"

Richard, grudgingly: "No. It's a gene."

"As a doctor of divinity, do you know of any biblical injunction to punish a woman as a witch because she is growing younger?"

"No."

"No further questions."

The district attorney had attacked Portia's defense of insanity by getting Richard to testify that there was reason to believe in witches, and he had had Richard add that there was no reason for Portia to attack Julia. But in the closing arguments the defense counsel maintained that Portia, a respected scientist, had been driven temporarily insane by an intense emotional response to a phenomenon that she blamed on witchcraft because she didn't understand it. The jury agreed and found her not guilty. People in the courtroom cheered the verdict.

Which meant, I saw, that it was the Widdicks who were on trial now, and our foundation. Richard had scored a grand-slam homer.

It was my turn at bat.

Chapter Eight

Many members of the family have kept diaries to tell about the years they will have forgotten before an R-Phase ends. Since everyone's adult life overlapped one of Robert's N-Phases, every diary mentions him. We must turn to Rosalind for the fullest account. She was the one who was closest to him and the one who most often quoted him directly. She is our best source for the first public knowledge of the R-factor and the way Robert dealt with it.

—GABRIEL (D) CHEN, ARCHIVIST

Aftermath, 2087 to 2090
By Rosalind (B) Harper Touhy

Robert—Dad—is a fighter who can adapt to change. Secrecy had served him well for a hundred years, but he wasted no time regretting its loss. He changed to tactics of pretended candor and to attack, claiming that the world could thank God for the Widdicks.

Fortunately he had a secret weapon: me. He sent a rocket to pick me up in Kuala Lumpur.

Ignoring screams from the media, which wanted to know all about multiple lives, he promised a press conference but delayed it until I had returned. Richard was being quoted everywhere, naming Widdicks who had begun new lives. Robert would not be rushed. After we had conferred, he scheduled the conference.

More than a thousand men and women with corders must have been in the auditorium. Nobody knows how many millions more watched at home or on public terminals. Robert stood at a lectern while I, at first anonymous, sat beside him. A microphone aimed at him from the ceiling was linked to instant-translation computers for media people from everywhere from Argentina to China. The mood of the media was threatening. Some were angry because they had been forced to wait three entire days until this big shot, Robert Hawkins, deigned to see them. All acted famished to bite into the biggest story since Lazarus was raised from the dead.

"I have been seeing a lot about myself and my family in the media the last few days," Robert said. He grinned. "I will explain several things and then answer questions. First, ask yourselves how old I look."

Of medium height, broad-shouldered and with a strong jaw, his brown hair touched with gray at the temples, he looked like a healthy man of about fifty.

"I am fifty-three years old," he said. "The reports that you have all carried that I am in my third lifetime are true. I was born one hundred ninety-seven years ago"—gasps and exclamations from the audience—"but I am fifty-three years old. Twice now, in my sixties, I have succumbed to amnesia and lived for thirty-five years or more as my memories disappeared. At the same time I grew younger. When these periods ended, I emerged with my faculties restored, but I was twenty-eight again, and all the other years had been erased. Today I remember my first twenty-five years and the twenty-seven years since 2059. The rest has been wiped out. Those years no longer exist for me. I can tell you a lot about what happened in 1910 but nothing about 2050 except what I have read."

Several questions were shouted, but Robert shook his head and waved a hand and said, "Later."

"I cannot emphasize too much that this is a painful experience," he continued. "Never mind the years of confusion in a ward for amnesiacs. The hard part is reviving to discover that the world you knew is gone and you have forgotten your wife and children and friends and all you did after the age of twenty-five. You are dead to all that gave life meaning in the lost years. In a very real sense you didn't live them."

Many members of the media still looked hostile, but I saw thoughtful looks on a number of faces. Robert pursued his point.

"I remember my first wife because I married young. Twice I have been crushed by discovering that she had died. I do not remember our having children or the pleasures of watching them grow. I do not remember the wife I married in my first new phase, or our two children, whom I have met as strangers in my second new phase. If this happens to me again, and I don't know whether it will, I will forget my present wife and our child. My wife knows that, for I have explained everything to her.

It's a good marriage, and it's painful to know that if I enter a fourth life, the present one will be lost to me. Last night I heard a news analyst state solemnly that it must be a great blessing to live repeated lives. I say it is a doom."

Robert sipped water from a glass on the lectern.

"The genetic cause of what has happened to me, and to some of my descendants, has been explained in the media. I should add that the gene we carry, which is called the R-factor, can be inherited by both males and females, but many of my descendants did not inherit it. There are people named Widdick who do not have it."

Aha! I thought. Suddenly he is a squid hiding behind a cloud of ink. He was talking about boys adopted by Widdicks, and their descendants, but he didn't explain that. Neither did he explain the mechanism of inheritance that could cause a child not to receive the gene. He wanted protective confusion to exist.

Robert went on to describe the Health Research Foundation, the companies it owned, and the genetic research it conducted. The companies paid their income taxes before funneling money to the foundation. Less than 1 percent of the foundation's income went to operate its clinic for people with the R-factor, and the clinic was used for research as well as for care of the victims. "You will hear more about that later." Genetic research had led to the products of New World Pharmaceuticals, and he named hormones from cloned genes that cured serious illnesses.

Time for questions.

"Why do you hide behind a false name?"

"I don't. Robert Hawkins is my name. I haven't been Robert Widdick for a long time. I chose a new name to avoid all sorts of complications, which you can imagine, if I kept the old name."

"Why have you kept the R-factor a secret?" someone asked.

"We haven't. It's on record with the Bureau of Genetic Standards. They have scanners look for it in the chromosomes of fetuses. We don't talk about it any more than we would talk about a brain tumor."

Again he had made the point that the R-factor was a bad thing to have, not something to be envied.

"Is the Richard Widdick who testified at the McVeigh trial your son, as he said?"

Robert sighed, involuntarily, I'm sure, before saying, "He is."

"After the trial, he named fifteen men who he said had the R-factor and had begun new lives or would do so. Was he right about them?"

"He was right about some of them but not all."

True. Richard's research must have been thorough, but he had included the names of a few of Robert's descendants through women who did not carry the gene. They had been at the family gathering last summer.

"Will you list the people who have the R-factor, whatever names they use?"

"Sorry. That's a private matter, up to each individual."

I heard a groan from some reporter who was thinking of the drudgery of finding fifteen people to ask them if they had the R-factor, and not knowing whether they would tell the truth. Most of them, I knew, would deny it. Like stud poker players, they would stand pat on the cards that showed, their false birth certificates and concocted credentials.

"Are the genetic maps of people who have changed their names on record with the Bureau of Genetic Standards under their new names?"

"I don't know. The Bureau will map the chromosomes of an adult upon request, but it's not required, except for identification in criminal cases. I haven't asked for a map myself. I am sure, however, that the maps of all children were taken when they were fetuses and are on record."

Much good that would do a reporter. The public, which included the media, could not search the records. The law made genetic maps available only to people directly concerned. A reporter couldn't work back from the name of a child with R and find the names of the parents on a birth certificate.

Before anyone could ask how fictitious identities were established, Robert said, "I now am proud to make an announcement that results from many years of research, for which cells of patients in our clinic were used. The R-gene codes for an enzyme that has been found only in persons who have suffered its effect. The enzyme was hard to find, because it appears naturally only in very small quantities. We can clone the genes and produce the enzyme in large quantities. The experiments were done largely by my daughter, Rosalind Harper Touhy, who is a professor of biogenetics. I will introduce her to explain the significance of her results."

I took his place at the lectern nervously. I can lecture confidently to two hundred students who respect my knowledge and authority, but I had never spoken before a crowd that thought of me as outlandish. Thanks to Richard, they knew that I was the mother of Julia and Portia and was living a second life.

"Before I proceed, I will add to my father's introduction," I said. "I was born one hundred years ago, in 1987, but in my new phase, I am forty years old."

While they digested the contradiction, I held up a test tube containing a clear liquid. "This contains the R-factor enzyme in solution. We call the enzyme juvenone." With classroom showmanship, I whirled the test tube around gently. "Its production in the cells is triggered by the adverse environment that comes with age, particularly in the ovaries of women and the testes of men. From those organs the blood carries juvenone to cells throughout the body and initiates further production in them. It acts on all cells by encouraging cell renewal, cell replication, but without the uncontrolled replication characteristic of cancer!"

I gave them a minute to think of the implications. Then I said: "Suppose a person has arthritis. The cartilage between bones is breaking down. If juvenone can be applied to the cartilage cells, the cartilage will renew itself, and the arthritic joint will return to normal. A liver could repair itself! So could a heart!"

How often had I chided myself for testing cloned genes in laboratory animals, during my previous phase, and not the enzyme that the genes produced.

"Rejuvenation?" a man in the front row shouted.

"Immortality!" a woman near him yelled.

I shook my head. "No. The enzyme cannot be applied to the brain without causing amnesia as the brain cells are replaced. In due course the brain will die. The enzyme must be applied repeatedly to other organs because their cells do not contain the gene that will cause them to produce more of the enzyme themselves. What we have is a cure for serious physical problems, but one that requires constant medical attention. I must add one caution. It works on chimpanzees, but it hasn't been tested on humans. That will be up to government agencies."

Robert stood up beside me and said we would take more questions. I had thought that the announcement of a miracle cure would divert attention from the repeated lives of the Widdicks, but the first question came from a man who asked, "How many people have the R-factor gene?"

"There are forty-eight," Robert answered. Somebody whistled. Richard had claimed there were fifteen. "Two more died in accidents." In other words, we were not superhuman.

"You say you have had five children. Most couples limit themselves to two. What justifies your extra children?"

"My wife is entitled to as many children as if she had married someone else." The question must have annoyed Robert, for he added testily, "Let me point out that the only source of genes to be cloned for juvenone, which will benefit everybody, is me and some of my children and some of their descendants."

He had overlooked the strain of altered bacteria, containing the gene, that was thriving in the laboratory. I said nothing.

"When will you ask the feds to test juvenone on humans?"

"Immediately," I answered.

"Have you estimated a market for it?"

"No, but it will probably be large," Robert said. "We will make it and sell it, but we will also license our patents, without charge, to others to make it. The price will be competitive." We had decided that a reputation as public benefactors was worth more than monopoly profits. Profits on competitive sales would be plenty.

One of the women reporters in the auditorium asked me, "Did you go through a period of forgetting everything, like the men?"

"Everything past the first time I was twenty-two years old." This was my chance to underscore Robert's emphasis on the cost of rejuvenation. "It lasted thirty years, not thirty-five as with the men, but thirty years is an endless time to be the prisoner of a mind that can't remember what happened an hour ago. I had been married at twenty-seven, so when I came out of the R-phase, I didn't remember my husband or children. Getting acquainted with them when they were grown, and strangers, was a poor substitute for knowing and loving them all along."

Strangely, to me, the news of a miracle cure won less attention in the media, at first, than the news of extra lives. Robert's face was everywhere. He declined to be interviewed for a Tri-D feature on "The Three Lives of Robert Widdick" on the grounds that all he knew about was less than half of his first life and only half of the last.

Most questions were directed to Joseph, our PR man. He tried to get across Robert's point that renewal was emotionally painful. People weren't interested. They envied us. Joseph refused to identify anyone but Robert and Richard and myself as people who had entered a new phase, and he denied, lying, that he was one of us, no matter what Richard had said.

The obvious people to question were men named Widdick. Two of them admitted without quibbling that they had the R. They did not guess how they would be pestered or how their children would be singled out at school. Others were trapped by implication if their fathers had disappeared from public view at the age of sixty. Their answer was given to them by Robert, who had assumed that experienced reporters would know where to look.

"I really don't know if I have the R-factor," they would say blandly. "It will be interesting to find out, won't it? No, I don't have a chromosome map. Never saw the need for one."

"Will you get one for us?"

"Sorry. I'm a great believer in the right to privacy."

Ben Widdick came forward voluntarily. He was twenty-seven, unmarried, and showed off his blond good looks and gymno muscles as a commando in the series "Daredevils of Space."

"I have the R," he confided to a zap sheet columnist, which was like tossing a lighted match into dry brush. "I'm proud of it. It doesn't affect my acting, which is what matters most to me."

"He's quick off the mark," Joseph commented sourly when he reported the resulting publicity. "Watch his career soar."

"Call him back here to see me," Robert said. "I will remind him that an enterprise as big as ours has good connections in the entertainment industry. I will point out the wisdom of keeping his mouth shut about other Widdicks. We can let him become a star or we can divert him back to summer stock."

Widdick is an uncommon name, but there were Widdicks who were not members of Robert's family. Most of them denied grumpily that they had the R. They were tired of being asked the same question by people who knew them. Surprisingly, a few who did not have the R claimed that they did.

"They live drab lives. They want notoriety and excitement," Joseph said. "Good. They will confuse matters."

Then somebody talked to Mercer Widdick, the adopted son of Leo. Mercer had never been told he had been adopted at the age of two, in 2035.

"I know about the R-factor," he said. "My father went into the R-Phase twenty-four years ago, when I was thirty. He had told me it was going to happen because he had an extra gene. I asked for my genetic map immediately, because I have a great wife and kids and don't want to forget them. I don't have the gene." He showed a picture of his chromosomes, with a short Y. "See for yourself."

That was a break for the family. If Mercer was the son of a man who had the R-factor but didn't have it himself, it meant that the causative gene could be lost.

But then an enterprising editor of a press association hired a genealogist to trace the descendants of Robert since his first marriage, to Helen, in 1913, 173 years ago. The drudgery of searching old records, and the cost of the time it took, succeeded in finding his first daughter, Jane, born in 1916, and some of her descendants. One of them was a man named Grover Hackbarth, a talkative retired insurance salesman.

"It's pretty far back, but I guess I'm some kind of Widdick," he told a reporter. "I sure don't have the R-factor," he said with a laugh, "or I would have gone into hibernation by now."

"Do you know anybody who does have it?"

"I suppose so, but it's hard to tell."

"Why is that?"

"Because I see a lot of the family at a summer place at Lake Miniwoc that Robert Widdick set up. We use first names, no last names, and there's no way to tell who has the fancy gene. Nobody puts on airs. Everyone is pretty much like everyone else, no smarter and no dumber. They talk about politics and their golf game and everything except the R-factor. I can tell you this, they're all great folks, R or no R."

"I suppose he thought he was doing us a favor, telling people we weren't supermen," Robert said. The trustees were meeting often. "What he did was tell the world about our summer resort at Miniwoc. One guard at the gate was enough in the past. Now we'll have to post guards around the perimeter to keep out media people and curiosity seekers."

"Who knows? We might become a tourist attraction." That was Tony Broadmead, trying to be funny. Robert glared at him.

Naturally we hadn't heard the last from Richard. Membership in his church ballooned with his notoriety, and his sermons took an uglier turn as he urged members to "do the Lord's work" in punishing us for our alleged sin. All of us delisted our commlink numbers. I was one of those who hired guards. Robert's home became a fortress. It became as hard to see him as the president.

Joseph did his best to turn attention to the cures expected from the R-factor drug, juvenone, by buying ads and arranging interviews with doctors. Many of them were as excited by a miracle cure, especially one that would require their constant supervision, as ants finding a ripe watermelon cut open for them. But other doctors saw their livelihoods in jeopardy. Who needed a heart replacement if a heart could repair itself? Coronary bypass operations would still be necessary, because juvenone could not prevent plaque from thickening artery walls. Kidney dialysis would become a forgotten nuisance as kidneys restored themselves.

A producer of technical tapes offered to pay me for exclusive rights to my scientific report. I declined. I would patent portions of the process and the altered bacterium, but the usual full scientific verification should be encouraged. Research scientists pleaded for samples of gene-spliced vectors or the enzyme itself. Not yet, I told them, not until my results had been published in a technical journal.

First I had to take my material to the Food and Drug Administration to apply for tests of the hormone on humans. I took it there myself. The director saw me immediately.

"Do you know what we have to do?" he asked unhappily. "We have to sidetrack everything else for your enzyme."

Ah! I thought. Pressure is already building up from people who are more interested in their aches and pains than in repeated lives. "Anyone with a new pharmaceutical product hopes for early approval," I answered.

My granddaughter Miranda Bannister Moley, who is amused by the fact that she is forty-six and I am forty, called me to report a hard day at the Bureau of Genetic Standards, where she was assistant director for records.

"The director told me the security office had checked your line through Julia to me," Miranda said. "He said he had checked my gene map personally and found that I had the R-factor on an X-chromosome, and why hadn't I reported it.

"There is no requirement to report it," I told him. "It doesn't affect my work. It is properly included on my map, as you discovered. Nobody has ever been told to flag an R-gene found in females. There are so many meaningless sequences of nucleotides on a chromosome that people probably didn't pay attention if they noticed it. I didn't like to think about it, because my daughter has it and my son doesn't. Out of millions of females, it has occurred only six times."

"Six!" he exploded. "Besides your grandmother, mother, yourself, and your daughter, who are the others?"

"My brother's daughter and my mother's daughter by her present marriage."

"Your brother's daughter? Do you mean a female can inherit this from a male?"

"Certainly," I said. It required a little thought, but it was elementary genetics. "If a woman has the R on one of her X-chromosomes and passes that chromosome to a son, he will have the R on his X and will necessarily pass it on to a daughter."

"So now we have to check the X-chromosomes of both males and females as well as the Y-chromosomes of males. We have to look for an Xf gene as well as a Yf gene. Hmmm."

"I could guess what he was thinking. More work meant a larger staff, a bureaucrat's dream. But he has looked up the bureau's records and he's mad at you. Expect a call."

I knew what to expect. When I saw the director in his office, he produced a copy of the report of 2036 by an investigator who had seen me while I was the doctor for men in the R-Phase. I had looked up our copy of it and had talked to a lawyer.

"You told our investigator that the Widdicks died after their amnesiac phase," he said accusingly. "You knew better. Did you know that lying to a federal investigator was a federal crime?"

"How do I know what I knew?" I answered. "I've forgotten those years completely. I may have thought that the two rejuvenations that had taken place were not a valid sample. Anyway, no harm was done, and if there was perjury, the statute of limitations ran out on it long ago."

He stared at me silently while I wondered whether a lawyer could argue successfully, if I had been charged with something to which the statute of limitations didn't apply, that I was no longer the same person. Finally he shook his head and said, "I can't get over how you look younger than your granddaughter Miranda. You can go."

He may have wondered whether even someone near the top of the federal pyramid, as he was, could tangle with someone as popular as I was becoming without his being reined in by the president's office. Popular I was, a celebrity despite all my efforts to live quietly, for I was the one who had developed a still-untested drug. "Don't grow smug," Robert warned me. At Cornell, where I usually had two hundred students for my lectures, twenty-one hundred had applied for next year's course. Graduate assistants would winnow them.

My children were celebrities, too, at school, and I didn't like that. I instructed them to say they didn't know anything about the R-factor or whether they had it. They grew impatient with fellow students who talked about it as well as reporters who pursued them, and they tried to live normal juvenile lives.

Late in the year there was a family event that was of more than personal interest. Miranda's daughter Angela married Marshall Widdick. Both were descendants of Robert, and both had the R-factor. They had grown to know each other during family vacations and, I learned, had lived together for several years.

The board was concerned about genetic defects in the children of cousins. I was curious about the possible effect of their having a child with the R on both sex chromosomes. We scurried to the records to find out how closely related they were.

The code for Angela was B-1-1-1-1. Adding the years of birth, that could be translated as Robert (B), myself (1987), Julia (2017), Miranda (2040), and Angela (2063). Marshall's code was A-1-2-1-1-2-1, which meant Robert (A), Harry (1925), William (1953), David (1981), Peter (2005), Colby (2036), and Marshall (2062). Angela was a fourth-generation descendant of Robert and his second wife. Marshall was a sixth-generation descendant of Robert and his first wife. What kind of cousins or stepcousins they were defied common terms, but I foresaw little danger of harmful recessive genes coming together in a child.

Angela let Miranda know as soon as she became pregnant, and Miranda let me know. When the fetus had its genes mapped in 2087, Miranda used her position at the BGS to get an immediate reading.

"It will be a boy," she told me, "with both Xf and Yf."

The genes were identical, although they were on different sex chromosomes. Genetic historians know about a vanished disease called sickle-cell anemia, in which identical variations of a gene reduced the oxygen-carrying capacity of red blood cells, while normal and variant genes on matching chromosomes did not, but conferred resistance to malaria instead. "The effect of paired genes may be stronger than with one," I said. "I have no idea what that could mean here."

The boy looked entirely normal when he was born in 2088.

Angela named her son Jason. Three years later she had a daughter, Ellen, who received her father's X and Angela's normal X by the laws of chance that govern inheritance. Without an R-factor, she would live and die a normal life. She would join cousins during the summer and learn that she was different from some of them.

It was too bad, but I am selfish about the R-factor and wished that I could be around to watch Jason grow up. As a child, he was stubborn and sometimes devious in getting his own way, and he was less boisterous than other boys, perhaps, but this was my first great-great-grandchild, and I was delighted with him. He showed no abnormalities.

Chapter Nine

Too many years have passed for us to match many events with their dates, but none of us will forget what happened in 2098. Vernon Hawkins, the son of Robert (C), was an eyewitness. So was Rosalind, but she was too upset to put it in her own memoirs. Vernon agreed that a personal account would be desirable, and he agreed to write it. We can be happy that he gave the background first.

—GABRIEL (D) CHEN, ARCHIVIST

The Crisis of 2098
By Vernon Hawkins (2099)

Juvenone, our wonder drug, may have been the greatest medical advance since vaccination, but it did not sweep the world. It would not restore youth to every organ and tissue in the body. Bones, yes; the nervous system, no. It was expensive and it worked slowly, and many people could not afford repeated visits to the doctor. Doctors had to be trained to apply it directly to the organ being revived and to use it in very small quantities. If the bloodstream carried it to the brain, temporary amnesia appeared as a side effect. That happened when a heart was being restored, because what the heart does is pump blood, but a sound heart was considered worth a spell of amnesia. To restore the liver, a doctor had to find the hepatic arteries and insert no more of the hormone than the liver could absorb without overflow. Delicacy in treatment was essential. Too little was better than too much, for supplemental juvenone could be injected, but an excess could affect the brain.

As we should have expected, much of the demand came from men who wanted flagging virility cured with treatment of the gonads and prostate. The Universal Health Fund, which would not pay for cosmetic surgery except for cases like disfiguring burns, would not pay to make men Casanovas either. Rich men could buy treatment; poor men could not. There was a new class distinction.

"I'm hearing angry rumblings of thwarted vanity," Joseph reported. "For every man who thanks us for juvenone, there's one who blames us for dangling a prize that the government won't let him have."

"Yes," Robert agreed. After a silence, he added, "People have to see us as the good guys. All right. We'll give juvenone for anything it works on at our clinics."

"We'll need more doctors."

"They'll welcome the training."

Personally, I found myself a celebrity. The R carried prestige with a lot of people. I was born in 2067, the only new male in the family since

Ben in 2060 and Marshall in 2062. By 2091 Ben, the actor, had enough celebrity to turn him into a peacock. Marshall was married to Angela and had the double-f child I had heard about. The three Widdick men born in the seventies had different names because they were the sons of men who had changed their names after going through the N-Phase. My name was Hawkins, but everyone knew that Robert was my father. Except for Ben, I was the only certifiable Widdick of marriageable age, and I was pursued by young women who didn't care about the effects of my extra gene. I yielded happily to the temptations they offered, but I was careful that we reap no bonuses of unexpected cases of our special brand of amnesia.

My cousin Ben proved enterprising. Perhaps it was because he had known personal tragedy, or perhaps it was just business acumen. His wife, a featured actress on his show, had died in childbirth, a rarity these days, when their son was born in 2088. The media showed pictures of Ben holding the baby and looking mournful. His ratings went up.

"I think she died to help his career," Alfred said in one of his bad jokes.

Ben must have wanted more children, but he declined to marry again, and he did not want any bastards. His solution may seem obvious, but I thought it was clever. He set up a private sperm bank, handled discreetly by a doctor who treated infertility. Children would be born to married women. They would be told that the sperm contained the R-factor but not who the donor was. He, on the contrary, insisted on screening the applicants for health, intelligence, and what came first for

Ben, good looks. Some women whose marriages had failed to give them a baby jumped at the chance to have one with the R. Since they were intelligent, they could guess who the natural father would be. They were willing to pay five times the going price.

Women who resorted to a sperm bank customarily secured the agreement of their husbands first. But one using Ben's bank did not. His scheme crumpled when a man named Woodring sued his wife for divorce after a prenatal test showed the R, and he knew he couldn't be the father. A reporter who covered the courts picked up the story, which instantly became big news.

I was working on enhanced intelligence at the time. A supplementary brain would be attached to the first, like a fetus in a womb with a good blood supply, but also with nerve connections. This could be done with chimpanzees, but they were still chimpanzees, not geniuses, which was what I wanted.

I envied Tony Broadmead, who had been to Mars and had decided that it would be impossible to make a colony on Mars self-supporting until water and air could be provided by transmutation of the elements. He had rebounded from discouragement and was building life-support systems for resorts on Antarctica and under the oceans. "Take a dog sled to the South Pole with an experienced guide." That was popular. "Watch pognophores sway in the blackest depths." That one was not.

I was with Robert, my father, discussing the dead end my research had reached, when Joseph called with the news about the divorce trial.

Robert guessed who was involved immediately. He pushed a button and told his commlink pickup, "Get me Ben Widdick."

Whatever Ben's defenses against unwanted calls might be, Robert's name blew them away. Ben's face appeared on the office screen. "Hello, Gramps," he said affably.

"I want the whole story," Robert replied curtly.

Ben looked puzzled. He was, after all, an actor. "What do you mean?"

"Don't waste time. This is urgent. How did you get this Woodring woman pregnant?"

"Are you prying into my love life?"

"I am not." Robert's "not" snapped like the crack of a whip. "You just implied that you are the father, as I had guessed. During the divorce trial the judge will insist on knowing who the father is to establish paternity for support payments."

Ben's smile broadened. "She doesn't know."

"Which means a sperm bank was involved, unless you've taken up rape."

"A sperm bank," Ben conceded.

"Then the court will ask the woman who her doctor was, and her doctor will be compelled to testify that you donated the sperm. The public interest outweighs the right to confidentiality in a paternity case."

"Oh." Ben's smile faded, then brightened again. "I was doing us all a favor. I was spreading the R-factor to males who won't have the Widdick name."

"Indeed. How far have you spread it?"

"Two more that I know of. There won't be any problems. The husbands knew their wives were going to a sperm bank. The wives don't know who I am, and the husbands don't want to know."

"How much did the women pay?"

Ben's figure was larger than I would have expected.

"All right. I'll tell you what you have to do. End the sperm bank operation immediately. Give me the married names of the women whom your sperm will make pregnant. Get this divorce suit ended before the Woodring woman herself finds out who you are. Pay Woodring whatever settlement he demands with your own money."

"My own money!" Ben yelped. "Are you trying to browbeat me?"

"If necessary," Robert said, still unsmiling. "Two of our companies are among your sponsors, and I have friends among the others. Your series could be canceled." He waited for the threat to sink in and added mildly, "Think this through, Ben. The public has doubts about us now. We can't have them saying the Widdicks are taking special advantage of their extra gene. And we don't want any surprises over who does have it."

Thanks to Ben, three boys with non-Widdick names were born in 2092. Besides Edmund Woodring, the boys were Guy Michaud and Pedro Escobar. We are watching them grow. No others have surfaced so far.

We couldn't keep the R-factor out of the news, of course. Academic noodles had to have their say. A math teacher got his name in the papers by saying we lived cycloid lives. "A cycloid," he explained, "is a curve, up and down like a series of arches, that is traced by a point on a circle that is moving forward along a line, like a tire on a car. When the curve is described by a point outside the circle, the curve dips below the line and loops backward before rising again."

"Let's put it on a T-shirt," Alfred proposed. "A circle with a curve dipping in and out of it all the way around."

"If that's a motion, it fails for lack of a second," Robert said.

Sometimes I thought Ben had had a good idea, if it had been kept under control. It appeared to me that a majority of the public resented the Widdicks. We were not only wrongly envied for our extra lives, but we were rich. Most people were poor, and some of them had no more education than an oyster.

As poor and ignorant people often do, they looked to strange cults and fringe religions for consolation for their troubles. Many of them came to believe Richard's charge that the R-factor was a satanic curse on mankind.

In 2095 eight-year-old Eric Widdick, A-1-1-2-2-1-1-2, was chased home from school by a gang that yelled, "Devil! Devil! Devil!" at him. They caught him and beat him up, leaving him to limp home weeping, covered with bruises and with one eye swollen shut. He knew nothing about the R-factor. His brother, Ira, three years older, knew who the boys in the gang were. Police weren't interested in what they called just a scrap between kids. We Widdicks knew it was more than that because they had called Eric a devil.

Robert's investigators learned that the assailants belonged to a youth group in Richard's church called Soldiers of Judgment. They and their parents had been filled with Richard's fanaticism. Similar groups existed wherever Widdicks lived.

At that time there were fifteen Widdicks of high school age or younger, although eight of them, including one girl, had other surnames. The trustees decided that all of them had to have armed escorts to and from school. We lived behind walls but were scattered and felt vulnerable.

"We could set up our own community," Alfred told the board, "but we have to leave home to work and to do a lot of other things. I can't see us surviving on handicrafts."

"We can't hide in a fortress somewhere without resigning from society and abandoning all we have built up," Robert said. "Where would you and Roz have learned genetics without college courses and graduate schools? We can't run our businesses with commlinks alone."

"Right, and there aren't enough of us to form an army if Richard stirs up a rabble against us. We have to depend on the law. We must be good citizens with a good reputation in our communities and do what we can to see that the police and politicians are friends of ours." Alfred chuckled. "Anybody here want to run for governor?"

Nobody volunteered. "Let's groom some of our younger people for politics," Robert said. "For the time being the best we can do for security is what we're doing, and keep our eyes open and our fliers fueled up. I'll have my people keep very close track of Richard's church."

Robert had always enjoyed politics, and various members of the family became involved with all three major parties. My mother, Becky, had become a national committeewoman of the Whigs. Covering all bets, we raised money for Republicans and Democrats, too, and we courted the wives of politicians by supporting their favorite charities. (They had hundreds to choose among.) In the election of

2096 I ran for Congress but lost. I have no doubt that my being a Widdick hurt me more than it helped. All three presidential candidates, however, supported an amendment to civil rights law that would bar discrimination based on "race, creed, color, sex, sexual orientation, or genetic pattern."

We thought of having our lobbyists and politician friends work to give us the right to new birth certificates when we entered an N-Phase. No more sham biographies. But we decided that it would be better to continue to have the R-factor show up, when it did, unexpectedly, under many different names.

We forgot where we were most vulnerable. Robert had just entered another R-Phase in 2098, at age sixty-four this time, when we found out. Leo had just left the clinic when Robert entered, and there were sixteen in amnesia now. We were talking about expanding the Juniper Falls Facility. A year earlier Joseph had suggested that we move it, because the Church of Sinners Repentant had bought a bankrupt summer resort five miles away for "summer courses."

"For all we know, they could train some of their hotheads in guerrilla warfare," Joseph said. "People can be violent when they follow what they call a higher law. I was born in 1973, and I can remember when I was young how antiabortionists set fire to abortion clinics."

"I'll be hanged if I run away!" Robert said. "Build a stone wall around our Juniper Falls place and put guards and guard dogs behind it."

We did so, and tried to feel secure, but the question of moving the clinic was raised again after Robert had entered it. Our agents reported that Soldiers of Judgment at the church camp were practicing military maneuvers of squad and platoon size. Alfred suggested using our resort property in Minnesota. We took no action.

Roz and I had rooms in the guest quarters at the clinic after flying up to visit Robert when it happened. She had been born eighty years before me, but she was my half-sister and we got along well. I had parked my flier beside the ambulance behind the clinic that afternoon before we went to see Robert. There was no point in telling him about current activities, because he wouldn't remember half an hour later. We relived his big press conference, which he would also forget eventually but was still alive in his mind.

"I knew I had entered R again when I found myself here," he said. "I'm keeping track of time. I started a notebook, with a message in front of it to remind me what it's for, and I make a mark each day when I wake up. It's discouraging! I figure I'll be in R for thirty-nine years this time. That's 14,235 days!"

"I'll probably be here with you in a couple of years," Roz said.

"And you have a shorter cycle, so you'll be out before I will. I'm glad we'll have the next N-Phase together."

About 3:00 A.M. a loud noise woke me up. I heard a shot, and dogs barking. Looking out the window, I saw that a guard had turned on a floodlight. A bulldozer had smashed through our wall and was moving toward the clinic building. A pickup truck climbed over rubble from the wall and turned to the right. Dogs barked furiously as they chased both vehicles. The bulldozer smashed through the front door and the walls beside it, then backed away.

Men on the truck threw firebombs at the walls of the building.

I slipped into a robe and hurried downstairs. Bells were clanging. Memories might have eroded, but nobody had forgotten the sound of a fire alarm, and Robert and several other men were there. Julia and Miranda joined them as Fred, who was the doctor now, appeared.

"Vern, call the county bomberos and the sheriff," Fred said to me. "They're firebombing the place. I'll make sure everybody's up and can get out."

One of the two guards, holding a rifle, ran up as I got on the phone. He understood immediately what calls I was making and said, "Hurry. They tossed a phosphorus bomb into the front hall, and people on a truck are going around the building dropping more bombs against the walls. This place will go up in minutes."

He ran toward the back door. I followed as soon as I had made calls to incredulous officials. We were seven miles from town, and it would take at least five minutes for law fliers and fire fliers to arrive. I found all sixteen patients as well as Fred, Roz, a nurse, a cook, a handyman, and two guards in the back hall.

"They may be waiting for us to come out this way," a guard said. "Then they'll shoot us. Get into that room on the side while I open the door."

He flattened himself against a wall as he pulled it open. Immediately a fusillade of shots sent bullets down the hallway. The headlights of the truck were aimed at us.

"Burn!" a voice shouted over a bullhorn. "You'll burn in Hell! Start burning now!"

Richard, I thought.

The guard fired quickly, twice, and both head-lights went out. As shots forced him back against the wall, the other guard turned out the hall light. I switched off the light in the room where the rest of us huddled. It was darker inside now than it was out-side, for although one incendiary device had been tossed too far from the building to set the wood afire, at least one other one had started a blaze. A red glare lit the truck and its surroundings.

"Some of them have spread out prone near the truck," one guard said. "It looks like two are still in the cab."

"Amateurs!" the second guard scoffed.

"They want grandstand seats for the show. For that they have to pay." The first guard leaned out far enough to aim at the cab. A bullet caught him in the chest near his right shoulder, and he screamed as he fell to the floor.

Robert had not forgotten how to use a gun. Before I could move, he ran to drop beside the fallen guard and seize his rifle. He fired from the floor at the cab of the truck. The second guard, still standing, fired at it, too. I heard glass shattering.

Suddenly the engine of the truck whirred to life and the truck turned to our right to drive away. Dark figures sprang up from the ground and ran after it to pull themselves up on it. The guard leaped through the doorway and fired at the retreating truck. This time there was no answering fire.

"Come on out before you burn up," the guard called to us. "Stay low."

Fred had four of the patients form a stretcher with their hands to carry the wounded guard outside. "I have medical supplies inside the ambulance," he told the guard. "I'll fly him to the hospital."

"Take some of the patients, too," Roz urged him.

I was afraid that our attackers might come back. "I can take some, too."

I made sure that Julia and Miranda and Roz were aboard my flier. The R-factor on X-chromosomes was too rare to lose. Only then did I think of Robert, my own father, and had him join us. He looked puzzled, as if he had already forgotten what had happened.

"Fire," I said to him in explanation. Leading him to my flier, I tripped over a dog that had been shot by men from the truck. At that moment the roof of the clinic fell in with a shower of sparks. Eight people remaining on the ground behind us as I followed Fred's flier into the air backed away from the flames and into concealment among bushes and trees. The county fliers swooped down as we left.

At the hospital the wounded guard was taken in for emergency surgery. The rest of us shared a few chairs or sat on the floor or paced the corridor in confusion. "Fire," was the only explanation I gave them. "We had to evacuate." Half an hour later I had to tell them again.

Two deputy sheriffs appeared. "What was going on out there?" one of them asked.

"Somebody firebombed us," I answered.

"I know, and shot at you, too. I talked to a guard. What's it all about?"

I told him and asked if he had caught anybody.

"A bulldozer ran a patrol car off the road. It headed toward Canada, but it won't get far. We stopped a truck that had a dead man, shot through the head, on the passenger side of the cab. The only thing the men on the truck would say is, 'The prophet is dead.' They sobbed and said it over and over, 'The prophet is dead.' "

Richard had led his own attack, I thought. When he was killed, his followers abandoned the attack in despair. He failed, but he will never know.

Ballistics tests showed that Robert's gun, not the guard's, had fired the shot that killed the son who had tried to kill him.

Chapter Ten

Robert discovered in his fourth lifetime that possession of the R-factor could have unexpected consequences. He had feared that the family would become an elite class, but he had not guessed that snobbery would arise within the family itself. One reason was frivolous, the other had substance. Just when it appeared that he had accomplished his goal of making the family secure, the family itself had put the future beyond his control.

—GABRIEL (D) CHEN, ARCHIVIST

Please, Enough!
By Robert (D) Porter (2179)

I must say I've lived a healthy life for the past forty-two years. Healthy enough that I may be granted a normal death from old age this time. It's the least that a man who was born 289 years ago has a right to expect, even though my present age in this year of 2179 is only sixty-seven. Sometimes I feel more like 289.

"You're probably good for three or four more lives," Jason told me recently. Jason upsets me. He is always confident that he is right. What's worse, he usually is.

"The way you say it, it sounds like a sentence of death," I groused.

"Birth is a sentence of death, but the family carries on."

"Who wants to be breeding stock?" I asked. His face took on the look of indulgent patience that infuriates me. "I just ran a computer check," I said. "I now have two hundred sixty-one living descendants with the R. Who are they? I hardly know these people. A lot of them are just names on a list."

I don't much like some of the ones I know, either, but Jason is the one who makes me grumpy.

My fourth go-around, as Robert Porter, started well in 2137. I was still trying to reconcile myself to the loss of Helen when Roz came to pick me up. I had read about her before leaving the clinic and was eager to meet a forgotten daughter who had meant so much to me.

My latest son, Vernon, had gone into R at the age of sixty in 2127, ten years before I came out of it. I would return to the clinic to visit him, but his report on Richard's attack and death left me indifferent, except that we were well rid of him. The gap in my memory made Richard someone I might never have known.

What a fine-looking woman! I thought as Roz said, "Welcome back, Dad." She looked just like her pictures, a tall brunette with calm blue eyes, high cheekbones, and a straight nose, and she had the vibrant good looks of youthful maturity. She embraced me. "The board has a training program for retros now, but I hope you'll stay with me."

"So I'm a retro?"

"Yes. A retrofit, like everyone who comes out of R and has to be brought up-to-date. People living their original lives are firsters. When they get uppity and call us antiques, I call them larvae."

"I hope they squirm." I said with a grin. "I'm glad to see my favorite retro, and I'll be delighted to stay with you."

We went to her car, a two-seater bubble without controls except for a panel of buttons, which she ignored. She said, "Home, James," and the car moved smoothly down the road.

"That was a voice code, with the receiver keyed to my voice," Roz explained. "Didn't you always want to say 'Home, James' to a chauffeur—or would you prefer a coachman?—and have him follow orders while you admired the scenery? I have voice codes for common destinations, and buttons to enter codes for other addresses. Now the traffic brain has us in its cuddly hands. We will be carried along at whatever speed the traffic will bear, and with no chance of crashes."

"What if the brain gets confused?"

"Built-in fail-safes. Do you want to watch a show while we ride?"

"No, thanks. I'd rather talk." Something was nagging at my attention because of its absence. "This car doesn't make any noise. Have we invented noiseless engines?"

"Almost. You'll hear some servos if you put your ear to the floor. We're riding on magnets, one in the car balanced with a magnetrack in the road. Trains have used them for a hundred years.

We sling unmanned craft into space with magnetic whirlers. People can't stand the acceleration, so they are launched the old-fashioned way."

"Subway trains?" I asked.

"Magnets."

"Aircraft?"

"No. Field strength weakens too fast." Roz smiled. "You rode a rigible once. You can look it up. They're used for cruises because they fly slowly enough for you to see what's below you. There are still paddle wheelers for Mississippi cruises, too."

I thought of noise, the crash of a hammer of a drop forge, but I asked about something more important. "What are you doing now?"

"I'm a ranchero." Roz laughed. "I run a bacteria ranch. We design genes to order and splice them into bacterial chromosomes to produce something useful. We breed the bacteria by the billions."

"I can see you at roundup time chasing bacteria with a branding iron," I said.

"The Patent Office prefers nucleotide charts. And I'm married. Don't look so surprised! I never was one for the spinster life. I am now Mrs. Julius Greenberg, and I have two children, Morris and Ruth. The kids spend most of their time playing with their robots and bios. Ruth has a two-headed kitten. Julius knows about you and can't wait to meet you."

"Rip Van Widdick goes back on display."

That was the beginning of my orientation, as Robert Porter this time. I had read a lot during a waiting period in the clinic, but much work remained to bring me from 1915 to 2137. The difference in our cycles made Roz six years older than I was, and she enjoyed acting like an older sister teaching a toddler to cross the street safely.

The big word these days was *bio*. Algae were altered to extract minerals like manganese from the sea. That was biomining. Then there were biosynthetics, biointelligence in computers, bio this, that, and the other. Juvenone kept a lot of people out of wheelchairs, but there were many other enzymes and hormones from cloned bacteria.

"We're very close to creating life in the lab," Roz told me. "We can synthesize nucleotides and string them together into tailor-made genes to splice into living chromosomes. The lab genes work, as if they had taken on life from the natural genes around them."

One day Roz asked me if I had read the testament by Richard in which he told about planning to bring down the family.

"No. Why should I?"

"I should think you should be interested in someone who tried to kill you."

"It's an accident that didn't happen," I said. "Richard means less to me than an accident I do remember, when a belt nearly dragged me under a saw. Someone cut off power just in time."

"We bought the testament for the archives when his church went broke and had an auction. I think you'll be interested."

I read it and did become interested in the way conflicts in childhood could twist a mind, even the mind of a Widdick. "He wasn't as smart as he thought he was," I commented when I gave the testament back to Roz. "Smart people don't become murderous monomaniacs."

"He missed little things, too. You saw the way he classified genetic combinations, XX with XY, XX with XYf, and so on. He didn't think it through. He missed the big ones that concern us now, XfX with XfY, XfXf with XY, XfXf with XfY, XfYf with XX, XfYf with XfX, and XfXf with XfYf."

"A man who memorized the begats should have gotten a kick out of figuring out the combinations, but I haven't thought about it either."

"You will," she promised. "You will."

I miss Roz. She was good company. For twenty-six years she soothed me when I became angry, and she gave good advice. We were fond of each other. When Roz went into R sixteen years ago, I knew what a death in the family must feel like. I had married Farah by then, and I was fond of her, but Roz was special.

My first hint that problems lay ahead came when Roz told me, "The trustees of the foundation want to interview you."

She had said "interview," not "welcome." I asked who the trustees were. She named them with the years in which they were born: Mario Ferrante, 2081; Ira Widdick, 2084; Roscoe Widdick, 2086; Patricia Hobart Ecton, 2093; and Ariel Colman Salzman, 2097. Five strange names.

"You'll notice that they're all firsters," Roz said. "They took control from the retros in a family vote. They say the retros take too long to learn how things work these days."

"I suppose the sun still rises in the east," I answered. "I doubt that people's motives have changed since the cavemen."

"But it would be hard for a caveman to learn how a computer works."

"Ben Franklin could handle it, and he was born quite some time before I was."

I was wary but determined to be firm when I was ushered into the boardroom. I would be dealing with experienced managers to whom I would look very young, but my native self-confidence was strengthened by what I had read about my past successes.

The five trustees were seated at a round table, with a seat left for me facing a portrait of myself, looking twenty years older than I did now. They stood up when I came in, which was a good sign, but only two of them were smiling.

"Please sit down," said the man at the head of the table, under my portrait. "I'm Mario, the chairman now. I'm a fourth-generation descendant of yours, and I greet you with a mixture of curiosity and appropriate veneration."

Whatever that meant. Probably not much. Certainly not enthusiasm.

He introduced me to the others: Ira, a seventh-generation descendant; Roscoe and Patricia, both fifth generation; and Ariel, also fourth generation. N-Phases of parents and grandparents, who started a new line of descendants each time, accounted for the differences.

"Roz is my great-great-grandmother," Ariel said. She was one of the two who had smiled when I came in. "Of course, I was older than she was when she came out of R and I met her, but I still liked to hear about how you raised her. It made you real."

That was it. Despite their knowledge of the effects of the R-gene, they had trouble believing that the man who had started it all was an actual person.

It was as if I had stepped out of my picture on the wall.

"Since you created the foundation, we have an obligation to you," Mario said. He made it sound as if I was an embarrassment that he had to deal with reluctantly. "We think we should elect you honorary chairman."

"Thank you, but honorary titles don't interest me," I answered promptly. "I prefer to be useful. Do you have anything else in mind?"

"We have discussed the options," Mario said. "For the time being, we think you should implement your orientation, which Rosalind has been so gracious as to undertake. Then you might like a hands-on job to become familiar with one of our subsidiaries."

Well! This fancy talk meant that he thought I might be good with a monkey wrench. "Do you still make things with steel and other metals?" I asked.

"Oh, yes. I happen to be fortunate enough to be president of New World Technology, which still owns a tool company. We have a branch that turns out authentic reproductions of antiques like fireplace tools. You might like that. Most things these days are made of glastics. Basically polymerized silicon compounds, you know."

He's patronizing me, I thought. Fireplace tools! Abracadabra compounds! I dismissed his piffle politely. "Perhaps I could be useful, at first, as a production consultant. Give me whatever ID I need to visit any of your plants and come up with ideas."

Mario stared at me as if I would try to diversify their glastics production into shaving mugs. "Do you really think you could use the methods of two hundred years ago to improve on what we're doing?"

"Two thousand years ago," I replied. "I know how to get people to do their best work, and I suppose you still use people along with all the computers. I have an instinct for opportunities and, as my record shows, for organization."

Roscoe, who was the other one who had smiled when I came in, laughed and said, "And you come on very strong. Maybe we should sic you onto Jason."

"Who's Jason?"

"Our double-f. He's very independent. He doesn't work for one of our companies. We buy computers from him. He comes up with better ideas than our own research staff."

The term "double-f" went over my head. I would have to meet someone who had chosen not to follow a guaranteed career in a family company, but not yet. All I knew about computers was what I had read and what I had learned from using computers in Roz's home. "The tool company is more in my line," I said. "Let me see what's going on there."

They agreed.

The manager of the tool company was not a Widdick, which made me wonder if the family's talents were running thin. The main products were still machine tools, like lathes and drills and saws and jigs and dies, but the work was all done by robots controlled by computers. That, I was told, was old stuff. Master computers controlled the others. What the human employees did was watch numbers and lights and squiggly lines on video screens. They were suspicious of a stranger named Robert Porter, who asked a lot of questions with the manager there to back him up, and they answered as briefly as possible. It soon became clear that they were bored with their jobs, bored with the company, and bored with one another.

I invited myself to have lunch with them in the plant cafeteria. All they talked about was last night's baseball game between the San Diego Padres and the Tijuana Hidalgos. Shades of the Athletics and the Senators! The important thing was that baseball was still popular.

"Do you ever play baseball yourself?" I asked a young man sitting next to me.

"Not since school," he answered. "If you aren't good enough to play pro, what's the point?"

"Fun."

"Funny to watch," he answered. But someone else said that he played in a pickup game now and then, and others said they were interested.

My first project was to set up a baseball league with teams from different departments and different plants. The goal was to build team spirit, and therefore loyalty to one another, and pride in the players' departments. Sometimes I played with one team or another myself. It was fun, although I didn't play often enough to regain my onetime skill. Other players liked to have one of the brass join them on an equal footing. Friendship with me translated into liking for the company. I couldn't think of any improvements in production methods, but there might be improvement in their supervision.

I spent most of next summer at the family's vacation retreat, Lake Miniwoc. The family had grown so large that different groups had to take turns, usually for three weeks at a time, and a hotel had replaced the cabins of the past. Some of the people knew who I was; some didn't know and didn't care. Why should they? They might be meeting one another for the first time. If the name Robert rang a bell and they knew I was their founding ancestor, they met me with initial awe, but that faded in the face of my youth and with familiarity. I talked to as many of them as I could, and I didn't like some of what I discovered.

"They say Jason is coming next week," I overheard one man say to another toward the end of the summer. "I'm sorry I'll miss him."

"Not me. You can have Jason."

I remembered having heard of Jason as a computer expert, and I called up his stats on the machine in my room. Jason Widdick, XfYf, born in 2088, son of Marshall Widdick and Angela Moley. Two genealogical codes, not one. He was A-1-2-1-1-2-1-1 through Marshall and B-1-1-1-1-1 through Angela. That made him my seventh-generation descendant from my first marriage and my fifth-generation descendant from my second. He was fifty in this year of 2138. Two children: Lena, XfX, 2113; Avery, XYf, 2115.

I saw at once that he had the R-factor on both the X- and Y-chromosomes. That was what double-f meant. Just as unusual was his descent from me in two lines. These facts did not tell why one man here was sorry to miss him and another one was glad.

Next week a young man swam out to join me where I lay on a float just offshore in the lake. He sat down beside me and offered his hand. "I'm Jason," he said.

I looked him over as I shook hands. He was tall, lean, and muscular, like a light-heavyweight boxer, with a washboard belly. A plain face, with clear blue eyes and a look of calm, even serenity. Brown hair, which might be wavy if it wasn't wet.

"You're fifty," I said. "I looked you up. You look twenty-five."

"Probably twenty-seven," he answered. "It's hard to tell. If you looked me up, you saw that I'm a double-f, with the R-factor on both sex chromosomes. The R-factor is no longer an unpaired gene trying to do the work of two but has its full effect, which is to repair cells constantly. It's like a computer program that can scrub an entire matrix and correct errors without losing anything held in memory. I grow older very slowly."

And I, as a single-f, was a Model T. Jason hadn't said so, but I understood that he was a new, improved model. "How long will you live?" I asked.

"Who knows? I'm the first. Sometimes I've wondered if Methuselah was a real person, not just a symbolic name, and was a double-f who lived nine hundred sixty-nine years. That couldn't be true, of course, because he would have passed it on to Lamech, who would have passed it on to Noah, and so on."

"I take it you read the Bible."

"Biblical myths and ethical concepts are important to our culture. I read a lot, and I remember things. One nice thing about aging slowly is that you have time to learn. Nobody can know everything, of course, and I don't know as much about what goes on inside a living cell as your daughter Rosalind does, but I can speak the technical language. My specialty is communications."

"I thought you conjured up new computers."

"Computers are communications devices. So is the brain, which is a biological communications center. Original thought is merely a way of integrating communications."

A pretty good merely. Jason's charmed life, amazing as it was, might endow him too generously with certainties. "Is there anything that isn't so nice about aging slowly?" I asked.

"I don't fit in. Your foundation takes good care of the single-f's, but it doesn't do anything for me except throw me in with people who are almost as strange. Some of the ones who know about me envy me. As soon as I discovered that I wasn't growing older and heading toward an R-Phase, I made plans to take care of myself. In about ten years I'll get a divorce and start over with a new name, just like the others, but I won't have lost any years or memories. I keep putting assets into a trust that I can cash in on at the right time."

I asked how the trustee would know he was turning over assets to the right person.

"My gene map. I filed it under my next name when I set up the trust."

"Won't the Bureau of Genetic Standards trip you on that?"

"No. The Bureau doesn't compare maps for different names unless a crime is charged or somebody is studying a genetic disease. The government is always trying to limit the right to privacy, to make it easier to control people, but Widdick influence with politicians has kept chromosome maps largely private. The Bureau has lost interest in the R-factor, except for routine records. The Widdick family doesn't cost the taxpayers a peso."

Nevertheless, it would be dangerous to become overconfident, I thought. In numbers the family was still little more than zero percent of the total population, and people are always ready to blame their troubles on minorities. Something occurred to me.

"If a double-f can happen once, it can happen again," I observed.

"Very good!" he said, as if surprised that I could think of the obvious. "It has happened. I had a double-f grandson two years ago. It will happen more often as single-f women marry single-f men. There's a fifty percent chance that any sons will be double-f. What we need is double-f women. That will happen, too, because a few of the men have the R-factor on the X-chromosome, and they can marry Xf women."

"If they happen to want to." I thought of another objection. "Inbreeding is supposed to be dangerous."

"Not if you marry a distant cousin. Ask Rosalind. Anyway, you can check the genes to keep undesirable recessives from coming together."

Talking to many members of the family, playing games with them, eating with them, I had decided that they were going soft. Now I had Jason to think about, too. Too many of the others had sunk into the swamp of self-indulgence that tempts the heirs of wealth. Never mind that all my stock, and Harry's and Jane's, in the Widdick Tool Co. had gone to the foundation when I set it up. Salaries were large, and savings went to investments, which multiplied over the generations. The trouble was that everybody had a cushion. A person who couldn't support himself with inherited income or with his own talents and drive could always be sure of being paid more than he was worth in a job with New World Enterprises. It left a sour taste in my mouth when I thought of how hard I had worked.

The day I met Sam, I called Roz to make myself feel better by talking face-to-face on our screens. "This prize young cub talks about nothing but the right clothes to wear to scramble parties," I complained.

Roz tried to console me. "You have the Pilgrim Father syndrome. Not many ancestors would approve of their descendants. Forget about Sam. Think about Wesley, who was elected governor at thirty-five. He's a good one."

"Maybe we can make Wesley president," I said. That made me cheerful.

In fact, Roz forced me to admit, the family wasn't so bad. Not many were dilettantes or full-time socialites. After the attack on our clinic, Leo had set up a foundation program to support education in math and science, steer young people away from woozy mysticism and popular superstitions, and teach them to look facts in the face. His son Werner, and then Marcia, two more names that were new to me, had kept it active.

Some Widdicks had spurned company jobs to see what they could do on their own. I met a teacher and a woman who sold robots and a man who recycled glastics. Even a poet. She ran a day-care center to pay the rent.

The farming branch of the family was the most independent. They had fourteen thousand acres of land in Canada, a gasohol plant, and food-processing plants. They owed nothing to New World Enterprises. I made sure that they contributed to the foundation, which would take care of them when they needed it.

Jason joined me regularly on the float, on which I

liked to sun myself after swimming and watch boats haul speed gliders past. He asked one day if I had noticed that the family had formed cliques.

"Yes. They're split between firsters and retros."

"Indeed, but it's more complicated. They compare their genealogical codes. They count the number of generations between you and them. The longest string of numbers wins. Did you know you have some eighth-generation descendants?"

"Really, Jason, I do try to keep up," I answered with annoyance. "Our esteemed trustee, Ira, has two sons here who are both eight generations away from me, and I know there are others. What a silly thing to boast about!"

We heard a yell from farther out on the lake and watched a speed glider that had dipped too low catch a wing in the water and do a cartwheel. The rider, a girl, managed to curl into a ball as she was catapulted into the air. She took two bounces across the water like a stone hurled from shore before she sank into it. In a minute her head emerged, and she waved to show that she was unhurt.

"That's Rachel, who's eighteen," Jason said, showing eyes sharper than mine. "I have high hopes for her. There are several single-f men the right age to marry her. I think she likes Brooks, who's four years older. Both have six numbers in their codes. That's a good start for a happy marriage."

I laughed and said, "I hope they would have more in common."

"Your family vacations have seen to that. They've gotten to know each other well."

The boat that had been towing Rachel's glider

circled to pick her up. "That's Brooks," Jason said as a young man reached over the side to pull her into the boat. He embraced her.

I was shocked. I know a lot of my attitudes are out-of-date, but to me people in minimal bathing suits look naked. Jason, however, nodded with approval and said, "Very promising."

"So you're a matchmaker, too," I said.

"It's too soon. There are five single-f girls younger than Rachel in the family. One is only three years old. In time some of them will look for single-f men. You see, Robert, people with the R-factor think they are better than others and don't want to marry beneath themselves."

"Ridiculous!" I exclaimed. "They're not better, just different."

"They are handicapped," Jason said, and he sounded sad. "Their R-cycles throw the men and women out of phase. Suppose Brooks marries Rachel. He's four years older than she is. She'll go into R four years ahead of him and come out nine years sooner. When he comes out, she will be six years older, thirty-one to his twenty-five. They may not like the change."

I wished I had a pencil and paper to work it out for myself, but I was sure he was right, as usual.

"It will be worth it if they have double-f children," Jason said. "I think they would be proud of that."

After I returned from the lake, I discussed what Jason had said with Roz. "There's no doubt that what Jason wants most is more double-f's," she said. "He wants company. He might get a bellyful. Suppose he took a strong dislike to someone and had to put up with him for several hundred years. Or married one! The bonds of romance would be stretched very thin."

"There aren't any double-f women yet, but Jason says there will be," I said with a sigh. "I'm going to go back to work and forget all this."

Naturally I didn't forget it, but I did keep busy. Most of our machine tools were designed to form glastic products. Therefore I had to know about glastics. They could be poured in sheets or shaped in molds before they were sawed and trimmed and drilled. I visited a number of customers to see how well our tools worked.

"They do the job," one manufacturer told me. "They're worth the investment."

Back at the plant I checked inventories of goods received and goods delivered and looked at the books. The books balanced, but fees for "expediting" made me curious. My investigation showed that the "expediter" was a front set up by the plant manager to pay himself extra money. A closed-circuit do-it-yourself kickback scheme.

Mario, as head of New World Technology, was satisfied to let the plant manager retire quietly and not go to prison when he repaid what he had cost the company. I could have become manager at the age of twenty-seven, but I preferred to be a troubleshooter and learn more about the rest of our businesses. Since *bio* was the big word these days, I started with Roz.

"You should see Ariel," she told me. "She is president of New World Biotechnics."

Ariel was willing to let me cover myself from head to foot in sterile overalls and visit the labs, but she said I ought to go back to college if I really wanted to know biology.

"I never went to college," I told her. "Just tell me what you're doing."

She gave me a printout of departments and branches and activities. "We've finally solved a problem for the women in the family," she said. "They've been unhappy because the fifty-fifty odds on which X-chromosome gets into an egg cell mean that half of their daughters won't have the R-factor. We've learned to go into the ovary and separate Xf eggs from those with only an X. When you consider that the chromosome contains about fifty million nucleotides, and they are all vanishingly small, picking out an X that has only thirty thousand extra base pairs is a very delicate task, but we did it. If you want a sex life, you have a sex life; if you want a baby, you go to the lab."

Neither of Ariel's two children had the R. She would have to wait until next time around.

"Jason will be pleased," I said. "He wants plenty of Xf women to pair off with Yf men.

"Do you read history?" Ariel asked. "Jason reminds me of those old race-purity nuts who wanted nothing but blond, blue-eyed Aryans." She looked unhappy. "I will admit that it would be nice to live for hundreds of years without losing your memory during intermissions."

I went through the company businesses, tightening operations here and there but doing nothing sensational. When Roscoe followed Mario and Ira into an R-Phase in 2146, I was elected to the board. By then I had married Farah.

That was the year Jason divorced his wife, who had come to look thirty years older than he did, and changed his name from Jason Widdick to Jason Achelis. He had begun learning Greek years earlier when he picked the name. True to his convictions, he had two Xf daughters after he married again.

That was also the year that Farah and I had a son, Cyrus.

Over the years I attended all of the family vacations and saw Jason each time. He was right about family attitudes. Children learned about the R-factor these days almost as soon as they learned that there wasn't any Santa Claus. When they grew old enough to understand what it meant, those who had it stayed together. Besides grading themselves on how many generations they were away from me, they gained prestige from the number of different ways they were descended from me.

At first there was only Jason's grandson, Melville Ferrante, the second XfYf among us. He could trace descent from me through six, seven, and nine generations through three different lines. Then came Jason's granddaughter, Elizabeth Ferrante. She had the same score and was vain about it. Naturally she married a Yf man, and they had two XfYf sons.

Rachel, the girl I had seen crashing her glider into the lake, and Brooks, the young man who had rushed to her aid, fulfilled Jason's expectations and married. Results: an XfYf son and an XfX daughter.

"Why couldn't they have had two sons?" Jason complained. "Their son could have double-f daughters, but their daughter can't."

"Maybe they wanted a daughter," I answered. "Lots of people do. Take a piece of cake when the plate is passed. I thought you were patient. You have the time for it."

"We won't fulfill our potential until there are double-f women to marry double-f men. All of their children will be double-f."

"Until the world is top-heavy with them?" I asked.

"No. We wouldn't let that happen. Population control is the key to a stable environment." He grinned and said, "Maybe we can man a space-ship with double-f's to explore the stars, which might take centuries. Meanwhile there's safety in numbers."

That was what I had told myself some two hundred years ago.

Jason looked at me slyly. "Ben Widdick has been in R and is out again, you know, as Ben (B) Cabot. I think he had the right idea nearly a hundred years ago. A sperm bank, but with an egg bank, too."

"Not on your life!" I objected vehemently. "Your premise that f's are better than other people is wrong. We're no stronger or smarter. Maybe less so. We haven't won any Nobel Prizes."

"I can see it now," he said. "Annual competitions to qualify for fertilization or implantation with the R-factor. Preliminary heats, runoffs, the works. A talent contest, filling a stadium for the finals." He raised his hands in mock defense against my rising fury. "The trouble is, people want to have their own children."

Single-f members of the family were never comfortable with Jason. Preferring to wait quietly for the inevitable, he said little about his hopes, but some of them joked about his breeding program. Everyone experiments with fruit flies in school, and they called themselves "Jason's froofs." A few of them rebelled and intentionally married non-f husbands or wives, or did so because Cupid is blind. Our third double-f man married a non-f girl he met in college, but Jason was mollified when he had two single-f daughters. Time was on Jason's side, and family gatherings promoted his hopes.

We had one hasty marriage a month after a midnight skinny-dipping party in the lake. Jason was gleeful.

My son Harry told me that he refused to be manipulated by a distant descendant. This time around he has had two non-f daughters. Jason was amused.

Jason was unconcerned when our governor, Wesley, failed to win his party's nomination for president. Jason thinks in centuries.

Our first double-f girls were born three years ago, in 2176, and two years ago. They will be nearly as old as Roz when she comes out of R next time. And we have twenty-three double-f males, five of them still in diapers. One is my second grandson by Cyrus. His brother, also double-f, was born four years earlier. I would like to watch them grow up, but I would forget.

Sometimes Jason acts like a man obsessed, showing me lists of who is the right age to marry whom. The list includes the retros.

Whose numbers also keep increasing. Fifty of my 261 living descendants are in the clinic now, including three for the third time. Roz is one of them. There are twelve other women. That girl Rachel is in R now, and so is Brooks. During my present long N-Phase I have met everyone now in R and have seen some go in and out. That has happened to all five of the trustees who met me. Now they can learn the pain of being a retro.

As Farah and I grow older, I think more often of Helen.

"This stuff that I started has taken on a life of its own," I complained to Jason. He took a new name again seven years ago and is Jason Hathaway now. "Tenth-generation descendants swim around like striped bass. There are two brothers who are descended from me four different ways. I no longer see the point to it."

"Survival of what you once called freaks," Jason replied. "You've accomplished what you set out to do. Now it's gotten beyond that." He looked at me speculatively, as if wondering how I would take his idea. "Life goes on and doesn't have to have a purpose, but if there's any cosmic purpose in the existence of single-f's, it's to produce double-f's. We fulfill the potential of the human race."

"You make me feel like a missing link," I grumbled. "Not halfway between apes and men but halfway between men and you."

He laughed and clapped me on the shoulder. "You're not a missing link. We're the same species. We pass the test for that by breeding quite normally with single-f's and non-f's. What you did was start bringing us toward what we should have been from the start. Our fancy gene was lying hidden all the time."

Jason dived off the float and swam ashore. He and his kind will inherit the world, I thought, and I am no longer needed.

I don't want to be around if I'm not needed. Not without Helen.

Like it or not, as we all know, Robert came back, not once but twice before he finally found the peace he wanted. In his last N-Phase he insisted on taking the name Widdick again.

Jason, who is now 410, is a rarity among us, an old man who looks old. Analysis of the R-factor gene with other genes that affect its activity indicates that he won't live again. We could say that Robert, who was born 469 years before he died, lived longer than Jason has, but only the first twenty-five of his years and the last ones ever meant anything to him. Jason says memories clog his mind. "My brain is full of dead files," was the way he put it.

Jason has written that he and Robert saw much of each other during Robert's E and F phases. "He studied history each time to support his view that we must not become an aristocracy, which invites revolution. His prestige made him a member of the board of the foundation, and he persuaded us to keep our ranks open to outsiders. He did not attempt to stem the flood of double-f's, but he used his status to channel the tide. I think he became contented."

There are thousands of us now. We have launched our starship. Its crew of ten men and ten women can live through the round trip. If they find a habitable planet, we may settle double-f's upon it. On Earth, nature will follow its own course.

—GABRIEL (D) CHEN, ARCHIVIST

ARTHUR C. CLARKE'S VENUS PRIME™

by Paul Preuss

VOLUME 6: THE SHINING ONES 75350-2/$3.95 US/$4.95 CAN
The ever capable Sparta proves the downfall of the mysterious and sinister organization that has been trying to manipulate human history.

VOLUME 5: THE DIAMOND MOON

75349-9/$3.95 US/$4.95 CAN
Sparta's mission is to monitor the exploration of Jupiter's moon, Amalthea, by the renowned Professor J.Q.R. Forester.

VOLUME 4: THE MEDUSA ENCOUNTER

75348-0/$3.95 US/$4.95 CAN
Sparta's recovery from her last mission is interrupted as she sets out on an interplanetary investigation of her host, the Space Board.

VOLUME 3: HIDE AND SEEK 75346-4/$3.95 US/$4.95 CAN

VOLUME 2: MAELSTROM 75345-6/$4.50 US/$5.50 CAN

VOLUME 1: BREAKING STRAIN 75344-8/$4.99 US/$5.99 CAN

Each volume features a special technical infopak, including blueprints of the structures of *Venus Prime*